# Planet Mail

# KATE PEARCE

ELLORA'S CAVE
ROMANTICA PUBLISHING

## *What the critics are saying...*

ಜಾ

**2006 eCataromance Reviewers Choice Nominee**

**5 Flags** "so hot [...] wonderfully written pulling you in and connecting you with not only the characters, but the planet and its plight. I highly recommend this book." ~ *Euro Reviews*

An Ellora's Cave Romantica Publication

www.ellorascave.com

Planet Mail

ISBN 9781419956621
ALL RIGHTS RESERVED.
Planet Mail Copyright © 2006 Kate Pearce
Edited by Briana St. James.
Cover art by Syneca.

Electronic book Publication July 2006
Trade paperback Publication June 2007

Excerpt from *Logan's Fall* Copyright © Beverly Havlir, 2007

This book is printed in the U.S.A. by Jasmine-Jade Enterprises, LLC.

# Content Advisory:

## S – ENSUOUS
## E – ROTIC
## X – TREME

Ellora's Cave Publishing offers three levels of Romantica™ reading entertainment: S (S-ensuous), E (E-rotic), and X (X-treme).

The following material contains graphic sexual content meant for mature readers. This story has been rated E–rotic.

S-*ensuous* love scenes are explicit and leave nothing to the imagination.

E-*rotic* love scenes are explicit, leave nothing to the imagination, and are high in volume per the overall word count. E-rated titles might contain material that some readers find objectionable—in other words, almost anything goes, sexually. E-rated titles are the most graphic titles we carry in terms of both sexual language and descriptiveness in these works of literature.

X-*treme* titles differ from E-rated titles only in plot premise and storyline execution. Stories designated with the letter X tend to contain difficult or controversial subject matter not for the faint of heart.

## Also by Kate Pearce

ℬ

Antonia's Bargain
Eden's Pleasure


## About the Author

ℬ

Kate Pearce was born and bred in England. She spent most of her childhood being told that having a vivid imagination would never get her anywhere. After graduating from college with an honors degree in history, she ended up working in finance and spent even more time developing her deep innner life.

After relocating with her husband and family to Northern California in 1998, Kate fulfilled her dream and finally sat down to write her first novel. She writes in a variety of romance genres, although the Regency period is definitely her favorite.

Kate welcomes comments from readers. You can find her website and email address on her author bio page at www.ellorascave.com.

### Tell Us What You Think
We appreciate hearing reader opinions about our books. You can email us at Comments@EllorasCave.com.

# PLANET MAIL

# Prologue
*Somewhere in deep space*
*Earth year 2406*
*Hammersford Village, Planet Valhalla*

හ

"By Thor's bones, how old is she?"

King Marcus Blood Axe stared in disbelief at the girl the village elders of Hammersford ushered into his tent.

One of the men stepped forward. "She is of age, Sire. She is eighteen."

Marcus walked a slow circle around the woman. She wore nothing but a heavy gold chain around her neck. Her lips and nipples were rouged; black kohl edged her wide, scared eyes. He took her chin in his fingers and made her look at him.

"Do you want to have sex with me?"

She blinked and peered over Marcus' shoulder at the group of men behind him. "I wish to help my village, Sire. I wish to bring favor to our region by bearing your child." She sank to her knees and handed him an ancient gold goblet filled with thick crimson wine.

Marcus stared at her bowed head. Despite her beauty, his cock remained unimpressed. How was he supposed to bed her if he couldn't even get hard? He'd grown weary of this endless game. At first, he'd enjoyed being offered the most beautiful of his people's women but now, at thirty-five, he felt old, tired and jaded.

He turned and bowed to the anxious men behind him. He had no choice. Ritual demanded he play his part. The

11

village was barely surviving on the edge of the Purple Desert. He had to give them hope. He drank deeply from the goblet of wine, wincing at the bitter aftertaste.

"I accept your gift and give you thanks for it. If this woman should bear my child, she and her village will be honored for all eternity."

The ritual words sounded hollow on his tongue as the men bowed their way out of his tent. He gestured reluctantly to the woman who knelt at his feet.

"Please, get up."

She stood, hands clasped together at her waist. Long brown hair curled to her hips and her head was adorned with a wreath of flowers. Marcus sat down and finished off the wine. He patted his knee. By Odin, he might as well get it over with. "Would you like to sit here?"

She nodded and came toward him, her breasts bounced as she walked. She balanced easily on his muscled thigh, one small, hot hand braced on his naked shoulder. He smoothed his hand down her back and she trembled like a frightened mare. Outside, the wind gathered speed, making the leather and silk hangings of the tent shudder and shake like a live animal.

"What is your name?"

"It is Lillian, Sire."

A beautiful name for a beautiful girl. Despite her age, he found it difficult to think of her as a woman. He understood why the village offered him their most prized possessions, their desire to enjoy the king's favor was reasonable. As rulers of the planet, his family held the ancient right to mate with any offered female and marry them if they proved fertile. Some of his ancestors had many wives. In more recent times, as fertile women proved elusive, they had difficulty in finding even one.

Lillian stared over his shoulder, her face a bland mask. He'd never really thought about how the women who were chosen to be bedded by the king felt about it. In his younger days he'd been too busy enjoying them to care.

Marcus licked his lips as his vision wavered. Lillian watched him through lowered eyelashes. A surge of heat settled in his belly and spread to his loins. Had the elders added an aphrodisiac to the cup? Did they believe the rumors that their king was impotent?

His cock hardened against her thigh. He barely resisted the impulse to rub himself against her. He slid his fingers into her hair.

"What was in the wine?"

"Only herbs to heighten your enjoyment, Sire, nothing more." He stared at her trembling mouth, wondered how his cock would feel as he thrust inside it. After a deep shuddering breath, which did nothing to calm the racing of his heart, he lifted her off his lap and set her away from him.

"Go, little one, I don't want to hurt you."

She fell to her knees and pressed her face to his thigh. "Please take me, I can't stand the shame if you leave me untouched. I'd rather face your anger if I fail to give you a child."

Marcus ripped open his loincloth and wrapped his fist around his cock. He squeezed hard, trying to restrain the raging desire to fuck her hard and fast. "What are you saying? Do you think I am a monster?"

"Everyone knows that you kill any woman who doesn't conceive your child." Lillian was crying so hard now that it was difficult for Marcus to make out her words. His gaze fell to her breasts which quivered with the force of her sobs. He sat back in his chair and pushed her away with his foot.

"I'm no monster. Leave me in peace." He desperately needed to attend to his cock before he came like an inexperienced boy.

Lillian got up and stood over him. Her tears had miraculously ceased. Her face was set. She placed her hands on the arms of his chair. The scent of her desperation and fear surrounded him.

"I'm not going anywhere."

Marcus' head fell back as she scrambled onto his lap, trapping him in the chair. She knelt over him and grabbed his cock. He could do nothing but groan as his body lost touch with reality and felt only the burning need to fornicate like a wild animal. He started to come as soon as she tried to lower herself down on him. His last thought as he lost consciousness was rage at being outwitted by a frightened woman and deep relief that he'd finally been allowed to spend his seed.

# Chapter One
*One week later*

ജ

"System overload. We are about to crash-land on this planet. Please take evasive action."

Jerked out of her stasis sleep, Douglass Fraser stumbled toward the pilot seat. This was supposed to be the easy part of her journey. She'd delivered her last scheduled package, used the last of her fuel and was meant to be on a free-trajectory return to Earth.

The soothing female tones of her ship's emergency alarms failed to dampen her fear as the ship hurtled toward a range of hills on the unknown planet below. Manually landing a damaged spacecraft was not something she did every day.

"Where the hell did that come from?" she yelled, not expecting a response but too overwrought to care that she was talking to a computer guidance system. "It shouldn't even be there!" Although the big purple planet wasn't on her charts, its gravitational attraction was affecting her trajectory and had pulled her out of the slingshot effect that should have taken her home. She grabbed the controls and reset them to manual. Despite her best efforts to remain horizontal, the ship dipped sharply to the right. Because the ship had no fuel left to burn the main engines, she couldn't pull away. She only had the ability to make slight course corrections to minimize the effects of landing. The wing grated on a sheer rock face and slowed her speed, sending the ship down at a less steep angle.

Douglass buckled herself into her seat harness and allowed the ship's emergency systems to cocoon her in some kind of foam. It started to harden around her as the craft rapidly dropped altitude.

"Ten, nine, eight, seven…"

She shut her eyes as the ship's auto-defense screens activated and shut off her view of the purple planet's surface. Dammit, she was only twenty-eight, way too young to die. And she had people who depended on her. She pictured her five-year-old son Danny smiling up at her, his face covered in chocolate, his sticky fingers clasped in hers. She *had* to get home. As the ship hit the planet surface with a screech and grind of tearing metal, she made herself a promise. If she survived, she was going to take a year off from the United Planetary Parcel Service and spend it lying naked on a beach.

When Douglass opened her eyes, she smelled smoke and charred circuits. She struggled to release herself from the crusty foam confines of the chair. By the time she clawed open the last restraint, flames licked at her boots. With all her energy, she crawled toward the hatch. Agony jabbed and seared her side. Had she broken anything vital during the impact? She fought the pain and managed to force the door open. Better to get out and suffocate than be burned alive.

She gulped in fresh air as she fell onto the soft purple sand. At least the planet had breathable air and an atmosphere similar to Earth's. Behind her, flames licked voraciously at the new source of oxygen. Heat blasted the back of her neck. She tried to stand, then clutched her side as the pain started up again.

She kept crawling, the sand warm and gritty against her palms. Sweat poured down inside her brown jumpsuit.

Ahead of her lay an ocean of swirling purple. She shaded her eyes and blinked as some of the dots melded together and became larger. A rescue party or trouble?

At this point she didn't care. There was nowhere to hide. She was injured and likely to die out here. The Space Academy had always stressed that staying alive was preferable to being heroic. Douglass struggled to her feet as the figures approached.

The largest of them broke away from the rest and brought his mount to within twenty feet of Douglass. She wasn't quite sure what it was the guy was riding, something between a chicken and a dragon. She stifled an inappropriate desire to laugh. This wasn't the time to insult her hosts by ridiculing their forms of transportation.

The man who dismounted looked enormous to her. He was cloaked, apart from his eyes, his face hidden behind a swath of fabric. Douglass stepped back as he came toward her. Damn he was big. Okay, she was only five foot four, but this guy towered over her. She reckoned he must be at least six foot five.

He stopped three paces away from her and unwrapped the cloth from his face. Douglass blinked hard. He had long, thick black hair and golden eyes, high cheekbones and a mouth that begged to be kissed. His cloak was lined with fur and his muscled chest was bare. Gold armbands accentuated his muscled biceps. He held out his hand.

"I am Marcus Blood Axe, king of this planet, Valhalla. Can you understand me?"

She automatically pressed her left earlobe to activate the embedded interplanetary translator but realized that even though his English was heavily accented she could make it out. To her fevered mind, he sounded Scandinavian. Perhaps the Vikings really had been the greatest explorers the world had ever known. She tried to restrain her unruly thoughts. She was already hallucinating, no need to make it worse.

"Yes. I'm Captain Douglass Fraser from the United Planetary Parcel Service. I would appreciate your assistance in contacting my people and reporting the accident."

He looked past her to the smoldering wreck of her craft. "Is there anyone else in there? Your pilot, your mate?"

"I'm alone. I'm the pilot, the first mate and the entire crew."

He didn't smile at her feeble joke. She pressed her hand to her side as another treacherous wave of agony caught at her breath. Behind her, the back end of her ship erupted, spitting forth a lethal rain of hot metal.

"Watch out!" the man roared, as he raced toward her. He caught her in his arms and supported her against his chest. Damn, the man was all muscle. Not a soft spot to lay her head. She wasn't used to being cradled in a man's arms. For a terrifying moment, she wanted to give up and bawl like a little girl.

"Are you injured?"

His quiet voice sounded loud in her ear.

"My ribs..." she hissed in pain as he gently ran his hand down her side.

He cradled her in his arms. "I will take you back to my palace. I swear I will take care of you. You will want for nothing for the rest of your life."

* * * * *

Douglass licked her lips and moved restlessly against the silk sheets. A soft male voice crooned to her and bent to suckle her nipple. Long hair slid against her breast as his warm, wet mouth moved over her flesh. Her legs were open. When she tried to close them, her thighs brushed another muscular body. Her breathing grew erratic as the suckling increased. Relief flooded her as fingers caressed her clit, stroked inside her brought her to climax.

"Shssh, quiet now, we'll attend to you. Just relax and open yourself to us, my lady. We wish to serve you."

A different voice this time. Larger, rougher hands on her breasts. Between her legs the gentle lap of a tongue, tiny licks in counterpoint to the harsh sucking. Douglass shivered as another climax threatened. A strong accented voice she thought she should know whispered over her.

"Aye, she is beautiful with her sex all plump and swollen, her nipples tight and wanting. You have done well. I look forward to joining with her."

She swallowed as something dripped onto her lips and tried to open her eyes. She tasted the sea and the musk of a man's semen.

"*Sa*," the man groaned and traced her lips with his wet cock. "I want to feel her mouth around my shaft more than I want to breathe."

Douglass tried to coax his cock into her mouth. Her nipples tightened beneath the sucking and the gentle licks to her clit increased. This was one helluva of a dream. She really didn't want to open her eyes just yet. Maybe after she'd come.

"Make her come, Sven. I want to see her."

Her pussy clenched around the four wide fingers that were thrust inside it. She whimpered, lifting her hips to take more. She felt the man kneeling beside her head move to straddle her chest. He drew her breasts together and pumped his cock between them as he pinched her nipples.

Douglass came hard, her lower body bucking off the bed.

"She is beautiful, Sire, especially like this."

The weight moved off her chest. "Aye. We have been blessed by the gods."

Douglass waited until the sound of the men's conversation disappeared. She cautiously opened one eye. She was still naked. The distinct scents of three men covered her skin. She'd let them bring her to a climax. Three complete and total strangers.

Shit.

She hastily shut her eyes as a movement to her left told her she still had company.

"I know that you are awake, my lady. I saw your eyes move."

Cautiously, Douglass peered at the naked man beside her. She inhaled her own musky scent and realized he must've been the guy with the magic tongue. He smiled at her, his long blond hair framing a face which would only improve with age.

"My name is Bron. I am going to wash you." He held up a silver bowl with flower petals floating on the surface.

Douglass just stared at him. "You don't have to do that."

He sat down beside her, placed the bowl on the table. "I like to wash you. I like the way your body responds to my touch." He reached for a washcloth. "I've enjoyed learning which parts of your body respond to which stimuli."

He leaned over her, his face intent and trickled water between her breasts. Douglass shivered as he slid the cloth over her already sensitized nipples. He cleaned away the stickiness with gentle touches as if he'd performed the service many times before.

The cloth slid over her stomach and around her hips. Her sated body relaxed into his touch.

"Where am I?"

Bron frowned. "Your ship came down in our desert region near the village of Hammersford. Luckily, the king and his companions, who had been visiting the village, saw the crash and came to your rescue." He touched her left side. "You broke two ribs and your left wrist."

Douglass slid her fingers over her skin. She felt a slight ridge of healed scar tissue. "How long have I been here?"

She sighed as Bron eased her thighs apart and knelt between them. For some reason, despite the recent stimulation, her body anticipated pleasure again. He dipped the cloth in the water and wrung it out.

"About one cycle."

Douglass struggled to remove her thoughts from below her navel. "How long is a cycle?"

Bron eased his fingers between her labia and spread them wide. As he stared down at her, Douglass noticed that beneath the white silk loincloth he wore, his cock was erect.

His voice was husky when he finally replied. "A cycle is twenty-eight days to remind us of a woman's fertility." He used the corner of the cloth to clean her aroused flesh. Although he was careful, blood thundered to her pussy and she grew wet. Had they touched her like this all the time she'd been half-conscious? Was that why she felt so comfortable being caressed?

Bron exhaled and slid one finger inside her. "You are always so eager and responsive. The king is truly blessed." He bent down and kissed her clit, making her squirm as he worked his finger in and out of her.

"Do you need help, Bron?"

Another familiar male voice intruded on Douglass' consciousness.

"You may play with her breasts, if you wish. I promised Sven I would be gentle with her after the last session. He and the king drove her wild."

Douglass waited until the second man sat beside her. He was as dark as Bron was fair. His long black hair was loose around his shoulders apart from three narrow braids at each temple. Like Bron he wore gold armbands and a skimpy silk loincloth.

"It is good to see you are fully awake, my lady. I am Harlan, the third of your servants." He squeezed her nipple. "Would you like me to sit behind you or by your side?"

Douglass simply stared into his slate gray eyes. Had she died and gone to heaven? Was this her fate to be sexually serviced for the rest of her life?

"My lady? Do you wish me to use my hands or my mouth?"

"I don't mind, whatever you wish. And my name is Douglass, not my lady."

He moved behind her, opened his legs wide and sat her in between them, her back to his naked chest. The wet silk of his loincloth stuck to her skin, his cock nudged her lower back. Bron moved too, sliding down between her legs, his finger still working her pussy.

"We would not presume to call you by your given name, my lady." Harlan said. "On our planet, a woman's name is only used by her mate. We are here to serve you, not mate with you."

Douglass wanted to purr as Harlan brought his hands around and cupped her breasts, his thumbs teasing her nipples.

"Be gentle with her, Harlan. The king doesn't want her overused. The ceremony will be tomorrow."

Douglass let herself drift on a cloud of sensuality. She'd never had two men in her bed before. She'd never had one man who seemed to think she was as sexually exciting as these men did. If they were softening her up before putting her to torture, they were making a good job of it.

She didn't feel used. How often did a twenty-eight-year-old parcel delivery girl get to be treated like a goddess? She glanced down at her body. Harlan's large hands cupped her breasts, Bron's finger pleasured her pussy, his tongue caressed her clit. Pleasure built and she arched her hips seeking the delights.

"Give her more fingers, Bron."

Harlan rolled her nipples between his fingers and thumbs sending a jolt of pleasure straight to her womb. Bron looked up.

"Is that what you want, my lady? I don't want you to be sore."

"Yes, please, more."

His fingers weren't as broad as the absent Sven's but they were long and flexible. He found her G-spot, held her on the pinnacle of lust. Harlan groaned in her ear and thrust his cock against her buttocks.

"Make her come. I want..."

Obligingly, Douglass splintered, her heels digging into the bed as she rode the exquisite sensation. Harlan grabbed her around the hips and spilled his seed down her back in short, sharp hot bursts.

When she opened her eyes, Bron had the cloth in his hands again. He smiled at her. "It appears that I'll have to start bathing you all over again. Please lie still."

Douglass struggled to surface from the overload of pleasure and grabbed his wrist. "Has anyone from my home planet contacted you yet?"

"If they had, why would you still be here? You are not a prisoner." Gently, Bron tried to remove her hand.

"Then what exactly am I?"

They both smiled as Harlan bent to kiss her cheek. "You are a gift from the gods and it is our job to worship you."

Douglass let go of him and laid back down as Bron started to wash her. Even if the planet Valhalla wasn't on the UPPS charts, surely her company had logged her disappearance by now? She bit her lip as Harlan smoothed fruit-scented cream over her skin. She knew Danny would be well taken care of by her mother and her friends but what would he be thinking? He was used to her traveling but she'd promised him that this last trip would be the longest she would have to take all year.

Was she wrong to enjoy the attentions of these men when her heart yearned to be back at home? She rolled over onto her stomach and buried her face in her pillow, her extreme sense of physical pleasure at war with her heart and her mind.

# Chapter Two

## ເຈ

By the evening of the next day, Douglass was alert
enough to realize that something momentous was going on.
Sven had returned and spent the night sleeping by her side.
Every time she'd tried to find out what was going on, one
of the men had distracted her with mind-blowing sex. The
weird thing was that none of them attempted to slide their
cocks into her even when she could tell they wanted to.

She felt like an athlete being prepared for some huge
event. She glanced across to the window where her three
men sat arguing around a table. Bron was the youngest and
the quietest, his blond hair framed an angelic face, his
lovemaking was as delicate and precise as his personality.
Harlan's striking dark looks mirrored his more intense
character. He seemed to be able to read her sexual desires
and act on them before she even realized what she needed.
He was taller and older than Bron but still not as awesome
in size as Sven, the acknowledged leader of the group.

Sven was the same height as the first man she'd met on
the planet, whom Douglass reckoned was the king. He was
at least six foot five if not more. He wore his red hair short.
She imagined it would curl if he allowed it to grow and she
doubted he would appreciate that. He was big all over.
When he touched her, she felt devoured, on the edge of a
roughness which called to some deeply hidden primitive
part of herself she hadn't realized existed.

She stared out of the window as the first of the planet's
two suns began its descent. Soon it would be dark and the
palace would come to life, soft lights illuminating hidden

walkways, silk drapes showing the shadowy forms within. It was time to demand some serious answers from her host. Why hadn't a rescue ship appeared after the crash? Was no one on Earth aware that she was missing? She thought of her son and her mother, would they think she was dead? So far all her questions had been smilingly swept aside or she'd been referred to the king who hadn't appeared in her bed since she'd regained full consciousness.

Douglass licked her lips. She knew he'd been there. His deep voice was even more familiar than the other men's. She'd felt his huge cock against her mouth, his hands caressing her breasts, his fingers buried deep inside her bringing her to climax after climax with the encouragement of his husky whispers.

Sven touched her shoulder. He should've looked ridiculous in the short silk loincloth but he didn't.

"My lady, there is something I need you to do for me."

Douglass eyed the golden cup in his hand with gathering suspicion. "I'm not drinking anything."

Sven sighed and came down on one knee in front of her. "We have discussed this and we feel you need to be relaxed for the ceremony. You are not of our land. Some of the celebrations might make you feel uncomfortable. We do not wish that to happen. We wish you only joy."

"What ceremony?"

"The ceremonial meeting between you and King Marcus. There will be many who wish to witness it. You need to be at your best." He proffered the cup. "This will help you relax and enjoy yourself."

Douglass stared at the cup and then leaned forward to sniff the contents. It smelled of mulled wine and herbs. A taste she remembered from her early days on the planet. "You've given me this before, haven't you?"

"Aye, when you were first given into our care. We wanted you relaxed enough to enjoy our attentions without fear." He reached forward and brushed her nipple with his thumb, smiled when it hardened. "Please do this for me."

Douglass gazed into his brown eyes and saw only a desire to be honest with her. She took the cup. What the hell. She hated formal occasions and avoided them like the plague. If this helped get her through a potentially embarrassing meeting, she was willing to give it a try.

Sven exhaled as she drained the goblet and handed it back to him. "Thank you, my lady."

He got to his feet. "We need to prepare you for the ceremony. Bron has already run your bath." He took Douglass' hand and led her to the huge sunken bath. Bron and Harlan already awaited her in the steaming water. She allowed Sven to help her and sighed at the warmth and the spicy scent of unknown flowers.

She floated across to Harlan who caught her around the waist. He bent his head and kissed her nipple as Bron's fingers slid between her buttocks. Caught between the two of them she enjoyed the sensation of being cradled between warm male muscled flesh, the feeling of being cherished and worshipped.

"You are beautiful, my lady," Bron whispered as his clever fingers stroked her sex and slid into her pussy.

"Aye." Harlan brought his head up and kissed her forehead. "And even more beautiful when you are climaxing." She leaned her cheek against his shoulder and watched his fingers work on her nipple.

Sven appeared at the side of the bath. "Remember, we have a lot to do. Don't make her come too often. We don't want her exhausted."

Bron removed his fingers after a last stroke of her clit. Harlan picked her up and brought her out of the bath. He laid her on the silken bedsheets and began to dry her.

"Why is this meeting so important?" Douglass looked up at Sven who waited at the side of the bed, his gaze fixed on her body.

He smiled. "Because you are."

"I don't understand." Even as she spoke the drug tugged at her senses, sending all coherent thought straight to her pussy. The rasp of the towel suddenly almost unbearable on her skin. Her breathing changed, as if she were running uphill. Sven dropped to his knees beside her.

"What's happening to me?" Douglass whispered. "You said the drug would relax me. I don't feel relaxed."

Sven took her hand, kissed her fingers. "We'll help you ride out the side effects. You'll need your strength and stamina to last the rest of the night." He squeezed her fingers. "Bron, bring the scented oil."

He knelt between her legs, the pot of oil in his hand. Douglass stared at him as her body heated and her pulse raced. He rubbed oil over his huge palms and placed his hands at her ankles. She shuddered as he slowly slid his fingers up the inside of her legs, stopping at the top of her thighs.

Harlan took a position close to her shoulder and began to massage the oil into her breasts. Every touch resonated as the drug spread within her blood and magnified every sensation. Sven's cock grew and thickened beneath his loincloth as he worked the oil into her skin. For the first time, it didn't seem enough to be satisfied, she wanted to give something back. As he moved over her, she ran her hands up his thighs. He groaned but did nothing to stop her exploration.

She brought her hands together, catching Sven's balls, cupping them in her palm. He thrust against her as if he couldn't stop himself.

"My lady, if you touch me like that, I will come."

Douglass pushed against his chest and knelt up. His chest rose and fell as she studied him. His cock, outlined in wet silk, thrust up to his waist. "Am I allowed to make you come?"

Sven nodded, his fingers reaching for her oil-soaked breasts. "Tonight, I believe you are allowed to do anything you desire. The king will understand."

Douglass drew the tip of his covered cock into her mouth. Sven groaned and pinched her nipples hard. As she sucked, she felt Bron's fingers at her pussy, following the rhythm set by her mouth. Harlan rubbed oil into her back and her buttocks, his finger probed her anus, slid inside.

God, she felt so open and filled at the same time. In the sane part of her mind, she knew she was behaving like a sex fiend but she didn't care as she took what they gave her and gave back to Sven. She almost gagged as his hand fisted in her hair and he tried to delve deeper into her mouth. The silk covering his thrusting cock contained his lunges, kept him chained and restrained to Douglass' desires.

He roared as he came, pumping thick and strong even through the silk. Douglass came with him, writhing against Bron and Harlan's fingers. The four of them collapsed onto the bed in a tangle of arms and legs. By the time Sven rolled off her, Douglass had recovered her breath. She smiled at Harlan and Bron whose loincloths dripped with come.

"I promise I'll get 'round to all of you, If you give me a moment to recover."

Harlan grimaced and stripped off his sodden garment. "We will look forward to it. Unfortunately, the time draws near for the ceremony. We need to get ready."

Douglass lay back on the bed and watched the men clean themselves. Her pussy throbbed and pulsed as they oiled each other and slid gold armbands on their biceps and wrists. She slid a hand between her legs and played gently with herself. Bron and Sven left their hair alone, Harlan braided his in one piece which hung down his back. It was like watching warriors prepare for battle. Naked, Sven walked over to her, a small box in his hand.

"There is something you might help us with." He gave Douglass the box and waited for her to open it. Inside were three gold rings. Douglass picked one up. It was way too large for her. Something was engraved on the side.

"These look too big for my fingers. Do you want me to put them on the three of you?"

Sven looked amused. "Aye."

Douglass crawled off the bed, her legs unsteady as she made her way across to the other two. The three men faced her. Leather straps tied tightly around their thighs and hips, and crisscrossed over their chests emphasized the strength of their oiled and toned bodies. She stifled a laugh at their serious expressions.

"This doesn't mean I'm married to all three of you, does it?"

"No," Sven said, "We are not worthy to become your mates. But it does mean that we will serve you when you need us."

Douglass studied the rings again. She noticed a spring catch on the back of each one. "These look too large for your fingers." She frowned. "Where on earth are they supposed to go?" She looked down. "Oh."

She sank to her knees in front of Harlan. His cock rose straight and thick from the thicket of black curls at his groin. Douglass licked his shaft, watched him grow larger. He reached down and took the gold ring out of her hand.

He showed her how to undo the lock. When he gave it back to her, she slid it carefully down over his shaft. A pearl of moisture slid down from the tip, Douglass licked it up.

"Don't tighten it too much yet," Harlan murmured.

Bron was next. He shivered as Douglass touched him. He was slick with moisture and it was easy to slip the ring on. Sven was harder, his cock so large that the ring was a tight fit even unlocked.

Douglass sat back on her heels and studied them all. If this was the last night she ever saw them, she would remember them like this. Their muscled bodies gleaming with oil, gold encircling their biceps, cock rings displaying the magnificence of their erections.

Sven produced another box. "Now it's your turn."

# Chapter Three

စာ

Douglass licked her lips and Sven turned her toward the mirror. Her skin was flushed pink, her whole body so sensitive that every touch made her shudder with desire. Harlan cupped her right breast and drew her nipple into his mouth. Bron did the same with the left. She gasped as waves of sensation flooded through her. She arched her back and rubbed herself shamelessly against Sven. He opened the elaborate silver box.

Douglass stared at the long gold pins in his hands that reminded her of hairclips. She cried out as Harlan set his teeth on her nipple and gently tugged. As he stretched her, Sven reached down and slid the clamp over the elongated tip. He tightened the clamp sending a sharp thread of hot need straight to her pussy. Bron drew out her left nipple and Sven clamped that one as well.

Harlan ran a fingertip over the gold and grazed her nipple, making her jump. "This one should be tighter. She likes it." She moaned as he tightened the clamp. They all studied her, their faces full of approval and lust. Sven cupped her breasts.

"If she was mine, I'd have her wear these all day so that I could suckle her and make her come whenever I chose."

Douglass stared at herself in the mirror as the men added gold rings to the clamps and chains to connect them together. How would it feel to wear these under her uniform all day, desperate to get home for her lover to release the ache? The weight on her nipples increased, the gentle tug became a deep insistent throb that made her long for the relief of a man's mouth.

She reluctantly drew her gaze away from her breasts when she noticed Sven taking something else from the box. She swallowed as he held up another set of golden and beaded clamps. Her body recognized what they were before she did and rewarded her with a thick rush of cream.

"Sit down, consort, and open your legs."

Douglass couldn't believe how much she wanted this experience. The constant stimulation over the past few weeks had opened her mind to new sexual experiments and she was eager to play.

Sven knelt in front of her and stroked her already swollen clit with his tongue. She closed her eyes as he sucked and nibbled her flesh, spreading her wide with his fingers to expose every sensitive part of her. The clamp felt cool against her heated skin. She gasped as he adjusted it until she could feel the blood pumping in her clit as loudly as her heartbeat. Harlan and Bron added the other clamps to her labia, increasing the sensations.

"Open your eyes and see how beautiful you are, consort," Sven crooned.

Douglass stared at her reflection. Her long black hair streamed down her back, held away from her face with a gold circlet. When she drew in a breath the heavy gold rings attached to her nipples tugged at her flesh. She could just see the beads hanging from the clamps attached to her clit and labia. She looked like a fertility goddess. She looked like a woman primed for a man's cock.

She leaned back against Sven's broad chest, nuzzled his nipple, bit it hard. "Do I please you?"

Harlan laughed as he wrapped her aroused body in a long velvet cloak. "You know you please us. It's the king you have to worry about tonight."

Douglass allowed herself to be led out of the suite for the first time. She breathed in the scent of ripening fruit and perfumed air before she was guided down beneath the palace walls. The sound of beating drums reverberated through the dark cave walls as they passed. At the huge doors, Sven paused and knocked hard.

Douglass gasped as the doors swung open to reveal a circular cavern, high stone walls disappeared into darkness above her. She could sense people watching from all sides. The center of the arena was a flat stone circle. Trees and bushes concealed the outer limits of the room. The drumming increased as Douglass and her escort walked forward and stopped in the middle of the circle.

Above them, on a stone dais, sat a masked figure, a glorious cloak lined with fur concealed his body. Douglass knew it was Marcus, the man who had invaded her dreams and her body and refused to leave.

Sven raised his hand and the drumming ceased.

"My King. We bring you your consort."

Marcus got to his feet, only his sensual mouth visible beneath the animal mask he wore.

"Display her for me."

Douglass shivered as Harlan took off her cloak, leaving her naked. A murmur of appreciation from the crowd startled her. Harlan and Bron lifted her arms high as Sven grasped her waist and lifted her off the floor. The three men carried her in a slow circle around the stones. They stopped when they reached the steps leading up to the throne where Marcus sat.

"Do you three wish to serve my consort and no other?"

Douglass stood alone as all three men knelt. She had to place a hand on Sven's shoulder to stop herself from falling.

"Aye, my lord, we do."

"You will protect her from danger, service her needs and keep her ready for me?"

"Aye, my lord."

Marcus stood up and bowed. "Then I appoint you as my consort's men for life. May you serve her as well as you serve me."

Douglass tried to catch Marcus' gaze but his mask shielded him too well. What did he mean about the consort thing anyway? Wasn't this just supposed to be a formal meeting?

"Show me my consort."

Douglass snapped back to the present as Sven moved behind her and gathered her breasts in his hands. "Her breasts are plump and heavy." He touched her nipples with the pads of his thumbs. "Her nipples are responsive. She loves to be suckled. It is easy to keep her nipples hard."

"Take off the jewels. Bron, suckle her for me."

Douglass held her breath as Marcus descended another two steps. She bit her lip as Bron drew her already taut nipple into his mouth and sucked. Sven held her close, the now familiar press of his cock plastered to her back, the unfamiliar rasp of the cock ring hard against her skin. She shivered and rubbed herself against him.

"Harlan, lick her pussy."

Sven came down on one knee and positioned Douglass over his thigh, opening her legs wide. Despite knowing there was a crowd watching, she had eyes only for Marcus. She was wet because he was watching. She was aroused because he willed it so.

The first rough pass of Harlan's tongue made her want to come. She stiffened in anticipation.

"Gently, Harlan. I don't want her to peak yet."

Douglass whimpered as Harlan resorted to baby licks and tiny touches. Marcus reached the bottom of the steps and stared down at her. She wondered how she looked, open to his gaze. Wondered if he wanted to push inside her and fuck her properly. Her body tensed at the thought. God, wouldn't it be wonderful to have a really huge cock pounding away inside her instead of this endless foreplay? She studied his thick shaft as he paused in front of her.

Marcus moved a step closer until he stood over Harlan. "Turn her around. Put her on her hands and knees."

With effortless strength, Sven turned her away from Marcus. She tensed as her breasts swung gently. One of the men pressed down on the small of her back making her butt arch.

"She is beautiful here too, my King." Bron's gentle finger slid past Douglass' tight anus. "With some more stretching you will be able to fit easily inside her."

Douglass tensed as she sensed Marcus circling her. From her low position she could only see his bare feet and the sweep of his magnificent cloak.

"Harlan, touch her clit and slide one finger inside her," Marcus commanded. Obediently, Harlan lay full length on the ground beside Douglass and did as requested. His finger felt cool against the hot pulse that pounded in her sex. "Sven, find a way to touch her nipples."

Sven knelt on her left side and reached for her breasts. Harlan continued to work her pussy. Bron stood behind her, his finger still embedded deep inside her back passage.

Douglass held her breath as Marcus crouched in front of her. She stared into the snarling animal mask as a peculiar sensual silence seemed to bind them together. With one hand, he swept the cloak back from his body. He was naked underneath apart from gold armbands on his upper arms. His huge thick cock rose straight as an arrow to his navel. Sweat gleamed on his muscular stomach.

"Suck my cock."

Douglass licked her lips and tried to move forward. The three men who touched her body so intimately held her back. She put out her tongue and just managed to lick the wet tip. Marcus growled low in his throat, grasped his shaft at the base and guided the crown against Douglass' mouth.

"Suck me."

Distantly she heard the audience roar their approval as he tilted his hips and surged into her mouth. He was so huge that she had to remind herself not to gag as he slid deep into her throat, filling her completely. She started to suck, enjoying the rough and smooth textures of his flesh, the wetness pouring out of him, his growls of approval. The drumming grew louder, echoing the pounding of her heart and her erratic breathing.

She tried to rock her body into the rhythm of her mouth but her captors wouldn't allow her to move. Her frustration mounted to burning point even as she soothed and pleasured Marcus' demanding cock. She wanted to come so badly she would've screamed if her mouth hadn't been full.

She moaned as Marcus fisted his hand in her hair and drew her head back, forcing her to release his cock. Still kneeling in front of her, he pumped his shaft with his fist. Her pussy clenched as she watched him work his cock. "Sit my consort up, Sven. I want her to have this."

Sven knelt behind Douglass and sat her down on his knees, her legs wide and open on either side of him. The music grew to a crescendo as Marcus stared at her. His face contorted as he came in hard shuddering waves, his come splashed her breasts and belly, her pussy. He leaned into her, rubbed his seed into her skin. She tried to close her legs around his hand and force him to make her climax but he wouldn't allow it.

"Take my seed. Give me children."

*What the hell did that mean?*

Marcus' quietly spoken words seemed to signal the end of the ceremony. Dazed, Douglass allowed herself to be guided up the steps to the throne. Marcus took off his mask to reveal the strong features and golden eyes already branded on Douglass' sensual memory. He reached out and flicked her nipple, bringing all her barely contained desires flooding to the surface. She stepped into his touch.

He smiled and moved away to sit on his throne. "It is time to eat. Sit with me." He patted his knee. Douglass stared down at him. He expected her to sit naked on his knee while she was frustrated and eat?

He snaked out an arm, brought her against him and rearranged her sideways on his lap. He brought a goblet filled with something alcoholic and apple-flavored to her lips. "Drink and try and relax. In the old days I would've been expected to fuck you in public and show the witnesses the proof of your virginity."

His deep voice definitely held a hint of a Scandinavian accent. She tried to relax a little, but his fast-recovering cock nudged her hip. "I'm not a virgin."

He smiled, displaying the dimple hidden low on his right cheek. "I noticed. No virgin would enjoy being pleasured by four men. You seem to revel in it."

Douglass struggled with reality for an unwelcome moment. Did he think she was promiscuous? "I've never behaved like this before in my life. I've never had sex with more than one man at a time before."

"Why not? Most women here are required to take at least three lovers." He fed her a piece of soft yellow fruit, which tasted like mango and something minty. When the succulent juice spilled from her mouth, he caught it with his tongue and licked it up.

"This fruit is called a love apple. Some women slide it into their pussies and then let their lovers eat it from them. Perhaps we should try it."

He stroked her nipple, drawing it tight between his finger and thumb. She shifted uneasily on his lap, trying to find a hard place to rub against. To distract him she asked another question. "Are there not many women on your planet? I don't think I have seen any, or is it just that you prefer all your companions at the palace to be male?"

Marcus resettled her on his lap, away from his hipbone. "There are very few females born to our race. Our scientists do not understand why. Most women are kept hidden away by their menfolk because they are so precious. That's why you don't see them serving at my court. I wouldn't be able to protect them from some of the more dangerous males."

Douglass leaned back until her breast grazed the edge of his cloak. "Can they not protect themselves?"

Marcus frowned as if she'd insulted him. "We are quite capable of defending our womanfolk. Why should they have to fight?" He drank from his goblet. "Why do your males allow you to travel so far from home?"

"Because they don't own us. Our planet has plenty of women on it. I choose to work for a living. I enjoy my job."

His smile widened. "You 'work'?"

"What did you think I was doing in the outreaches of the galaxy? Having a vacation?"

He wiped his mouth and concentrated on her face. "I wondered if you had been set adrift as a punishment or were running away from someone."

"Nope, I was doing my job. Haven't you ever heard of the United Planetary Parcel Service?"

He shook his head. "We rarely see any spacecraft here, only the agricultural transports that come to pick up our grain and produce for market."

Douglass swallowed hard. Was that why no one had come to find her? Her last scheduled delivery had been to the outermost planet in the UPPS system, a planet that had only been visited twice in the last ten years. Information was still sketchy about this whole area of space. She'd only taken on the assignment because of the huge financial bonus attached to its completion. Planet Valhalla certainly hadn't registered on her ship's guidance systems or charts. The king brushed a finger across her brow.

"Do not look so worried, my consort. We will continue to try and contact your people."

Douglass studied his arrogant features. She wasn't sure he believed her about her job. He seemed to find the idea of her choosing to work slightly amusing. Her mind wasn't functioning well enough to embark on an argument about feminism. She needed to attend to other pressing matters first. Greatly daring, she picked up a piece of fruit, placed it between her lips and offered it to Marcus. Surely he'd kiss her now?

She sighed as his lips met hers and melded into his. He kissed her with a deliberate slowness, a conscious taking possession of her mouth. She pressed herself shamelessly against him, whimpering as his long fingers fondled her breast and tried to rock her pelvis into his side.

He drew back and studied her. "What is it you want, my consort?"

She squirmed closer to his taut, muscular frame. "I think you know."

He gestured at the three men who sat at their feet eating their supper. "Do you wish one of your men to serve you?"

She laid her hand on his chest. "No."

He raised an eyebrow. "They do not please you?"

Douglass dug her nails into his skin. He didn't even flinch.

"They please me. They just don't please me enough."

He removed her hand from his chest, kissed it and gave it back to her. "Then what is it you want?" He held her gaze, his golden eyes steady.

Douglass decided she had nothing to lose. She'd already cavorted naked in front of a room of complete strangers. She'd allowed four men to sexually stimulate her at the same time. Why couldn't she just be honest and say what she wanted? She drew in a deep breath.

"I want two minutes alone to take care of myself."

His golden gaze narrowed and then he smiled. "Unfortunately, that's not part of the ceremony." He snapped his fingers. Sven looked up.

"Sven, my consort needs your services. Please make sure that she remains in a state of arousal but don't let her come." He maneuvered her around to sit with her back to his chest and pushed his knees wide, exposing her pussy.

"No…please." Douglass moaned as Sven licked her clit.

Marcus cupped her breasts and she shuddered. "What is it, my consort?" His cock stirred against her back. She realized he wore a cock ring around the base. "Perhaps I should put you on your hands and knees again so that you can suck my shaft and Sven can play with your pussy."

"No, please. I want you."

Sven stopped licking her. Marcus leaned over her shoulder to stare into her face. "What did you say?"

"I want you."

He looked politely confused. "I don't understand."

Douglass gritted her teeth. "I want you inside me."

"Sven can put his fingers inside you."

Douglass briefly closed her eyes. "I want your cock inside me."

"And why is that?"

"Because I've been dreaming of you touching me since the moment I saw you. I've been wondering what you would feel like naked against my skin, thrusting into me, coming inside me."

His mouth descended over hers in a voracious kiss that left her shaking. He got to his feet and threw her over his shoulder. The guests roared their approval as he slapped her hard on the backside.

"Then I'll take you to bed and fuck you." His satisfied murmur reached her ears as she struggled to readjust to her sudden distorted view of the world.

He carried her out of the hall and up another set of narrow stone steps. She had a perfect view of his tight butt muscles as he climbed the stairs. She blinked as he stepped through a sliding panel into what she assumed was his bedroom. His huge bed was covered in silver-gray silk sheets and fur coverings. Candles covered the walls and a fire burned in the stone chimney.

Douglass clutched at Marcus' muscled biceps as he swung her back onto her feet. He walked her toward the massive bed and lifted her onto the middle of it. She tensed as he followed her down, his body pinning her to the mattress.

He grinned and allowed his stiff wet cock to glide over her stomach. "What did you say you wanted?"

Beyond shame now and desperate to feel every one of the nine inches of his shaft, Douglass opened her legs. "I want you to fuck me." She risked a kiss on his shoulder. "Now. Please."

He reached up, gripped her wrists in one hand and drew them over her head. Her body arched like a bow, presenting her breasts to his mouth. His expression darkened as he studied her.

"You consent to our joining then?"

Douglass quivered as his teeth grazed her nipple. "Yes. Didn't I just say so?"

He knelt over her and reached for something above her head. Cold metal fastened around her wrists, keeping her hands trapped above her. His cock grazed her cheek as he adjusted the chain, she turned her head and licked his wetness into her mouth.

"Thor, do that again." He thrust harder, pushing the crown of his wide shaft between her teeth. She circled the sensitive slit and dipped her tongue in. One of his hands moved between her breasts and stroked her nipples.

God, she was so close to coming. Douglass had never had an orgasm from breast stimulation alone but, hell, she was going to now. As if he had read her thoughts, Marcus stopped touching her. She strained against the restraints as he removed his cock from her mouth and crouched back on his haunches between her legs.

He stared at her exposed pussy, flicked her swollen clit with his fingertip. "The first time I pleasured you, you were barely conscious, but you still flowered for me. You still dripped cream onto my fingers and into my mouth. Every time I touched you, I wanted more. I wanted you to wake up so that I could have you completely."

"I remember your touch. I remember the taste of your cock against my lips. I knew you weren't there when I came fully back to consciousness." She smiled boldly into his eyes. "None of the others made me feel the same as you did."

He wrapped a hand around his thick glistening shaft and rocked forward onto his knees. He touched her sex with the crown of his cock.

"Is this what you want?"

Douglass tried to lift her hips and force him inside her. "Yes."

He circled her opening with the tip. "This?"

A spasm of frustration shook her so hard she ground her teeth. "Inside me."

She almost screamed as he sat back again and considered her. She watched in desperate fascination as he smeared his right index finger in his come. He slid his finger deep inside her.

Her interior muscles tried to clamp down on him but he kept still and gave her nothing to work against. He coated his other index finger as well and guided it inside her back passage. Impaled between his hands but unable to come, Douglass felt close to weeping.

"What do you want?" Marcus asked again.

Douglass glared at him. "I told you. I want you."

He looked down at his swollen cock and smiled.

"What do you want me to say?" she almost screeched as he held her on a sensual high wire. He leaned in and licked her nipple, then licked it again, the light stroke adding to her confusion and frustration. When he raised his head she was panting.

"Have you ever begged a man to fuck you, Douglass?"

"No, I've never been that desperate."

"How about now?"

She wanted to say no so desperately but realized she couldn't. She was caught in a sensual web too powerful to break with the word no. Her body sensed she was on the brink of the most amazing sexual experience of her life.

"Marcus, king of Valhalla, I beg you to fuck me."

He removed his hands from her completely. "Then why didn't you say so?"

Douglass gasped as he thrust inside her, the size and thickness of his cock a brutal invasion that her body welcomed and feared at the same time. She knew he wouldn't consciously hurt her, but he was huge. She fought to relax around him but immediately got caught up in the biggest orgasm of her life.

Marcus didn't wait for her to finish, he just carried on thrusting, carrying her higher and setting off a series of orgasms that sent her body into spasms of delight. When she opened her eyes, he was braced over her. She was amazed to see she'd managed to take all of him inside her.

"Will you release my hands? I want to touch you."

He shook his head as his fingers moved over her, finding and centering on her clit. "Tonight I pleasure you. It is your right as my consort. Tomorrow will be soon enough to attend to me."

With his cock still buried inside her, he reached down and grasped her around the waist. "Let's see if I can turn you over without losing my place." She drew her knees up as he slowly rotated her onto her hands and knees. The chains attached to her wrist bands obligingly swiveled too.

"Whenever I thought of you naked in my bed, this is how I wanted you most." He knelt over her, his hips lined up behind hers, the soft scratch of his furred stomach against the soft skin of her back, the weight of his balls tucked into the curve of her clitoris and mons.

He stretched out, moved her hands until they grasped the head of the bed. "I want to shoot my seed deep inside you. I want to hear you scream when I release myself." He settled one massive hand over her breasts, the other over her sex. His hips pistoned forward, slapping his flesh against her buttocks. His cock seemed to grow larger and threatened to hit the neck of her womb with each deliberate stroke.

Douglass could do nothing but hang on and endure the pounding. His fingers pinched her nipples and her sex sent fresh waves of excitement to her already beleaguered senses. She felt herself build toward another climax. Her world narrowed to Marcus' harsh groans and the insistent smack of his groin against her buttocks. He bucked against her one last time and released hot streams of come deep inside her just as she climaxed around him.

He sagged over her, his massive frame covering her completely. He stayed like that for several minutes until his breathing evened out. Reaching up he released her wrists and rolled over onto his back bringing her with him. Douglass cuddled against his chest and closed her eyes. His fingers slid down to touch her soaked pussy. She opened one eye.

"We're not finished for the night yet, my consort. Although I won't make you beg again," Marcus murmured. His cock stirred against her stomach.

Douglass closed her eyes and began to pray.

# Chapter Four

ဢ

Sunlight sliding through the shuttered windows woke Douglass. She tried to stretch her sore muscles. Marcus' hands curved possessively over her breast, the fingers of his other hand cupped her mound. How many times had they had sex? She groaned at the sensuous thought. At least five, although it might have been six if you counted his coming into her mouth as she came into his…

Marcus sat up, tipping her over onto her back. He looked down at her, the dark shadows of his unshaven cheek a foil for his golden eyes. To her horror, his cock was already erect and thrusting upward. She groaned as Marcus parted her thighs and knelt between them. He touched her sex and she jumped.

"Do you think you are too sore to take me again?"

She shuddered as he parted her labia. "I know I am."

He leaned forward, braced on his massive forearms. "But you will take me anyway because I wish it." He slid gently inside her and held still. "I will be quick, I promise you. Just lie quietly and let me attend to you."

Now that he was inside her, Douglass felt a little better. She reached up one arm and wrapped it around his neck. He nuzzled her neck as he rocked his hips. Out of the corner of her eye, Douglass registered that the door to the suite was open and that Sven, Harlan and Bron stood watching them. Marcus increased his pace and she forgot the other men and clung to his moving body as he squeezed another climax out of her.

He kissed her breasts as he slid out of her and got out of bed. "She is all yours, men. And she was everything she promised to be." Marcus slapped Sven on the back as he passed him. "See that she bathes and eats. I'll return this evening. Make sure she is ready for me."

Douglass sat up and held one of the sheets against her breasts. "Excuse me. I am here. I can make my own decisions as to how I wish to enjoy my day."

All four men turned and stared at her. Sven bowed. "You are the king's acknowledged consort. You owe him your obedience."

Douglass shot a glance at Marcus who stood impassively waiting for her reply. She wished she hadn't drunk so much of the fruit-flavored wine last night. Perhaps then her recollections would be clearer.

"Excuse me? When did that happen? I had sex with him. Wasn't that the point?"

Sven frowned at Marcus. "Did she agree to your joining?"

Marcus inclined his head. "Aye, she did. Ask her if you doubt me."

Douglass scrambled to the edge of the bed. "I agreed to have sex with you, not to become your…"

"Consort," completed Marcus, a satisfied tone in his voice.

"What the hell does that mean?" Douglass thought it sounded rather permanent. Dammit, she should've listened better. She shouldn't have agreed to drink the dammed wine Sven had given her. She got off the bed, and nearly fell over. She glared as Marcus winked at Sven.

"You are the king's consort," Sven said. "His sexual partner, his lover, the potential provider of his heirs."

Douglass gaped at him. "Are you saying we're married?"

Sven bowed again. "Nay, the king would only be obliged to marry you if you become pregnant with his child."

"Ha! I'm protected against pregnancy, I have a patch..." She searched the soft skin of her inner arm where her contraception patch was situated. "Where the hell is it?"

Marcus answered her. "I believe the patch was damaged because of your injuries. The physicians attempted to reattach it but it was impossible."

Douglass frowned as she mentally tried to recall her monthly cycle. She couldn't get pregnant from one night, could she? Dammit, she had the first time.

"So consort means I'm some kind of a disposable wife?" Her attempt at sarcasm seemed to be lost on the men.

"If that is the correct terminology used on your planet then, yes."

Douglass glared at Marcus. "And for how long am I supposed to be this consort person?"

Harlan looked confused. "For the rest of your days, or until the king grows tired of you. It is a great honor."

Douglass walked over and poked Marcus in the chest. "Grow tired of me now. I have a life on another planet. I have a job. I can't stay here!" She realized she sounded shrill.

He smoothed his hand down her arm. "You can't go anywhere until we fix your ship or contact your people. Perhaps you might consider staying and enjoying what I have to offer you until that moment comes." He stared into her eyes. "I would consider it a great honor to make love to you until then."

Her body melted at his sensual tone. She could stay here and enjoy the attentions of four men. One of whom was the greatest lover in the universe or sit alone in a hotel waiting for her world to contact her. Marcus stroked her breast. Her nipple hardened.

Douglass looked him in the eyes. "Do you promise to let me go?"

"I would rather wait until your ship arrives and you can make your decision then."

"But you wouldn't stop me if I decided to go?"

He sighed. "I swear I will not stop you. Is that answer sufficient to stop you pestering me with questions?"

Douglass grinned at him and turned to Sven. "Where's the bath?"

As she lay in the bath, which was more like a small swimming pool and could easily fit four adults, she contemplated Marcus' words. He had been quite insistent about her asking him to make love to her. She should've realized there were different cultural implications to what he'd meant. They had gone on about that at the Space Academy at great length.

Despite her worries about Danny, Marcus was right. She wouldn't be here very long and she had his assurance that she could leave when she wanted to. At least she knew her son was loved and well cared for. Despite having never met his father, Danny was a happy child who thrived in the company of others. At five, he had no real concept of time. She smiled at the thought. She might get back and find that he hadn't even missed her. There was nothing she could do to hasten her departure so why not enjoy herself? She'd worked hard to support her family for the past five years. Maybe she was due a vacation.

Harlan soaped her breasts as Bron washed her hair. She relaxed into their hands.

"I wasn't sure I would get to see you guys again after last night."

Harlan cupped his hands and trickled water between her breasts. "Why would you think that? We were chosen to serve you. We bear your mark." He took her hand and wrapped it around his cock where she could feel the curved edge of his cock ring.

"You don't have to wear that all the time, do you?"

He smiled as his cock grew between her fingers. "Only when we are with you. Usually we will not all be with you together. We take shifts so that you are cared for night and day."

Douglass frowned as Bron lightly kissed her shoulder. "But doesn't the king mind?"

"Why should he? He chose us personally to care for you. We consider it an honor."

"That's the bit I don't understand. Most men I know would run away screaming if asked to pamper a woman for more than five minutes."

"Because women are scarce on our planet, and touching one, and being touched in return, is considered an honor. And it shows how much our leader trusts us not to dishonor what is his." Bron's cock brushed her hip as he combed lotion through her wet hair.

Douglass opened one eye. "I'm not 'his'. I'm a person not a possession."

Harlan laughed as he flicked her nipple with his tongue. "Bron meant sexually. We are allowed to service you in any way you desire as long as we don't come inside you."

51

"And am I allowed the same freedom?" Douglass climbed out of the bath and Bron wrapped her in a thick towel. Absentmindedly she flicked at the water droplets shining on his muscled chest.

"You can gift us with anything you want except taking our seed in your womb. That is the king's privilege." Sven sat on the end of the bed and laid a tray of food in front of Douglass. She realized she was ravenous.

He poured her a glass of apple-scented wine. "Our task is to keep you in a state of arousal so that the king can successfully fertilize you."

Douglass winced at Sven's words. "You make me sound like a broodmare." She pictured Marcus moving over her, the hot stream of his seed deep inside her. "Why does he need me? Surely the king has many children?"

Silence fell around her. Douglass studied Sven's face. "The king has no children? Has he not tried to...?"

Harlan took Douglass' glass out of her hand and refilled it. "The king is not at fault. It is difficult for anyone to conceive on this planet. Our scientists do not understand why although, as Sven mentioned, there were not many women here to start with. And over the last thirty years, many families have left the planet to avoid the fighting over their daughters."

Suddenly Douglass lost her appetite. No wonder Marcus had been so nice to her. His whole future and the future of his people could depend on her giving him a child. She pulled the towel from her hair and rubbed vigorously. She wasn't sure if she wanted that kind of pressure. It sounded as if the king were sterile and that no one dared to admit it. What would happen if she didn't succeed? What would happen if she did?

Perhaps it would be better not to mention Danny to the king. It might sound as if she was rubbing his lack of children in his face. Or, even worse, he might conclude that as she had a child, she was highly likely to conceive another one and despite his promise, not let her leave. She couldn't stay here. Dammit, she couldn't risk having sex with Marcus again either. Every cell in her body screamed a protest.

She tried to sound casual. "What about the king's previous consorts? Does he chop off their heads if they don't produce a child?"

"That is a vicious rumor, consort." Sven growled.

Bron took the towel away from her and started sorting through her tangled hair with careful fingers. "The king has never taken a consort before. You are the first."

Douglass closed her eyes as Bron kissed her throat. Should that make her feel better or worse? Speculation that the king might be infertile didn't completely rule out the threat of pregnancy. Could she hold out until UPPS came to rescue her? Surely she wouldn't be here that long and she had three guys to make it up to her in other ways. Too tired to think, she smothered a yawn as the food settled in her stomach. Sven got off the bed.

"Harlan and I will leave you to sleep with Bron."

Harlan kissed her fingertips and then wrapped his silk loincloth around his hips. Bron persuaded her to lie down beside him. His hand settled over her breast.

Sven spoke from the door, his voice oddly distorted. "Make sure she is ready to receive the king when he returns. He likes her wet."

Douglass winced. "He makes me sound like a fish."

Bron's chuckle was smothered against her shoulder. "My lady, go to sleep. The king will expect you at dinner tonight and you must be ready for him."

\* \* \* \* \*

Douglass sat at the king's right in the Great Hall. Despite her protests, she'd only been allowed to drape a skimpy piece of cloth across her hips. The rest of her remained bare to the gaze of the hundred men who ate with them. The concentration of stares on her breasts felt almost physical, especially as Marcus continually caressed her breasts and nipples making them taut and tight.

As the only woman there, she should've felt vulnerable but she found the men respectful and almost worshipful. She felt like a goddess. Beneath the scrap of silk, her sex grew warm and wanting as Marcus stroked her skin and fed her morsels from his plate.

"The men would probably like me to display you to them again."

Douglass almost choked. "What do you mean?"

He gave her a sidelong glance that shouted sex. "I think you know. Sit you on my knees and open your legs wide so that they can see your pussy. Work my fingers deep inside you until you come and then thrust my cock into you."

Douglass suppressed an urge to cross her legs. "Surely if you are the king, you can decide how much of me you want them to see?"

He slid his hand up the inside of her leg, stopped at the edge of the damp silk. "I like them to see you wet and ready for sex. I don't want them to see your face when I fuck you and you come for me. That's between us."

"Thank goodness for that," Douglass muttered. Thinking to change the subject she asked, "How long have your people populated this planet?"

"If you believe the tales of our bards, for many hundreds of years." Marcus signaled to a harp player to move closer. "Our legends tell of men who conquered both Earth and space."

Douglass listened to the unfamiliar language of the harpist's song. Even her translator couldn't decipher it. She was glad Marcus' people had reverted to the common interplanetary language of English. "There was an ancient race on Earth called the Vikings who were legendary seafarers and discoverers of new lands. Your language and culture reminds me of them."

Marcus nodded his head. "Aye, I have heard that from other travelers." He raised his cup to her. "Perhaps there is some truth in it." He paused to feed her some bread. "Your name sounds like that of a man."

"Douglass?" She smiled. "It can be used for either sex. Although you are right, it's more usually a guy's name. I'm called after an ancestor of mine who traveled from Scotland to America in the nineteenth century."

"I've read of those times. Traveling across continents was once as perilous as traveling through space. Your ancestor must have been a brave and courageous woman."

She checked his expression and could see no hint of amusement. "She was a brave lady. She married and had ten children." His smile disappeared. Too late she remembered his childless state. "But that wasn't unusual in those days…"

"Douglass, there is no need to explain yourself." He brought her hand to his lips. "I'm not so desperate for a child that I can't bear to have them spoken about."

He released her fingers and got to his feet.

"Would you like to take a walk with me around the palace? I can explain the areas which are safe for you to visit."

Douglass reclaimed his hand. "I was beginning to worry that you intended to keep me in my bedroom for the rest of my time here."

"Don't give me ideas, consort."

Marcus patted her arm as they progressed down the hall. When they exited, high sandstone walls rose on either side of them, shutting out what remained of the natural light. The floor was covered with blue and red mosaic tiles. Shaded oil lamps threw out muted pink shadows as they passed.

"You will need to keep within the palace precincts," Marcus said. "A fertile woman is considered a great prize and there are men who would do anything to get hold of you."

"How do you know I am fertile?"

Douglass faced Marcus as they passed into a more shadowed walkway. He shrugged and slipped his finger between her legs. She shivered at the brush of his calloused finger pad against her waiting sex. "Because while you recovered from your injuries, you bled from here."

Annoyed at herself for blushing, Douglass kept walking. She hadn't bothered to use artificial contraception methods to completely stop her periods. They'd always been irregular anyway. Chemicals never seemed to agree with her and it wasn't as if she was in a stable long-term relationship anymore. The patch she wore when she flew off planet was designed to work with her body's natural biorhythms to avoid pregnancy and still allow her to menstruate.

Desperate to avoid Marcus' amused gaze she noticed Sven and Harlan hovering a discreet distance away. Marcus smoothed his hand over her buttocks.

"It is nothing to be embarrassed about, my consort. It is a great gift. Many of the women on this planet no longer bleed."

Douglass had never thought about the rhythm of her monthly cycle as anything other than a nuisance before. For a people threatened with extinction, she was sure it was different. Marcus settled his arm low around her hips and turned her to the left. A shower of white petals rained down on her unprotected head as they passed through a corridor of living rambling plants which crisscrossed the ceiling and hugged the walls.

She inhaled the soft perfume, delighting in the velvet-soft brush of the petals against her aroused skin. Marcus bent his head and licked at a petal stuck to her breast.

"You are beautiful, my consort. Your skin is as soft as the petals of the *ozan* tree." He eased a finger between her legs and slid inside her. His thumb settled over her clit. Unhurriedly he tasted her mouth as his finger slid in and out at a steady regular pace. She grew wet, the sound of her juices loud as he pleasured her.

Just when she was close to coming he moved away. "There is something I want to show you at the end of this passageway." Douglass allowed Marcus to take her hand and lead her out of the semi-darkness.

The sound of water beckoned as they came out into the brightly lit circle. A life-sized statue stood in the center of a pool. It looked as if it had been carved from ice and was tinted a delicate pink which made it seem alive.

"These are my parents."

Douglass studied the huge muscular warrior and the woman he held in his arms. The warrior's head was thrown back as if he were caught in the throes of passion. He held the woman in front of him, one hand kneaded her breasts, the other rested on her belly. As Douglass moved closer she realized the woman was impaled on the man's huge cock, her eyes closed in ecstasy.

Marcus moved up behind her, the heavy shaft of his erection poked at the small of her back. "Do you like it?"

"I'm not sure if I'd like to see my parents at such an intimate moment but it is a beautiful sculpture."

Marcus chuckled and brought his hand around to torment her breast. "My father was a lusty man. As a child, it was impossible to avoid their lovemaking. I was always popping up at the wrong moment."

"And it didn't frighten you?"

"Why should it? To worship a woman, to be loved in return. It's the most natural thing in the world."

She bit back a smile. Danny had never seen her have sex with a man. Possibly because she hadn't had sex with anyone since he was born. It was probably why she was enjoying Marcus and her servers so much.

He took her hands and placed them on the low marble wall surrounding the pond and sculpture. His knee nudged between her thighs widening her legs, forcing her weight outward and onto her hands.

"I've always dreamed of bringing my consort here and making love to her." He tested her readiness, found her wide open. She felt his cock slide into her from behind. "They would have liked you. You are everything a consort should be, warm, willing and wet." He rocked gently into her, wrapping his arm low across her belly to ease her back into his thrusts.

Douglass allowed herself to be drawn into his rhythm, felt her climax build and clenched around him with strong, slow, voluptuous ease. Dammit. She couldn't allow this. With all her strength, she pushed away from him. With a curse, he came against her buttocks. His teeth nipped her neck as he gave a final shudder. The erotic image of his parents gazed down at her as the fountain continued to pour water over their shining forms.

"Why did you pull away?"

"I just remembered I can't have sex with you."

"Yet you took your pleasure before you denied me mine." He frowned down at her. "You are my consort. You agreed to mate with me."

Douglass pushed her hair out of her eyes. "But I didn't understand what that meant to you. And I thought I was protected."

"In your culture it is acceptable for a woman to have sex with a man and not give him children?"

She forced herself to meet his gaze. "Of course it is. Women choose who fathers their children. They are the ones who have to bear them, after all."

"You do not want my children?"

From the quietness of his question, Douglass realized her answer was important.

"At the moment, I do not want any man's children. It's nothing personal."

Marcus didn't seem mollified. "My lovemaking offends you?"

"No, it's perfect, it's out of this world, it's…"

He smiled at her. "Then I will wait until you are desperate for me as you were last night. Perhaps you will change your mind and beg me to make love to you again. Perhaps you will learn to welcome my seed."

Douglass simply stared at him as he held out his hand. His arrogance was unbelievable.

"Marcus, do you understand what I just said?"

"I understand, consort."

He took her hand, tucked it into his and started walking again. "This area is safe for you to visit as are all the levels above it. It is dangerous to go any lower. The kitchens, guard rooms and storage facilities are below. There is no reason for you to visit them."

Wary of his sudden acquiescence, and still primed for a fight, Douglass frowned. "What about going outside? I couldn't stand being cooped up here until the rescue ship arrives."

Marcus turned to face her, hands on his hips. "That could take many cycles. And why would you wish to go out? Most women prefer to stay quietly in their homes."

"Maybe they do here, but where I come from, women have a perfect right to go wherever they want."

He sighed. "I understand that our ways are different to those you have known. But to venture outside without an escort could risk your life."

Douglass lifted her chin and stared right back at him. "I need exercise. I need to feel the sun on my face and the wind in my hair."

"If I promise to look into the matter, will you promise to remain inside the palace?"

His gaze shifted from her face to her legs and stayed there. In the soft candlelight, Douglass guessed he could see the wetness of his seed trickling down the back of her leg. He gave a soft exclamation and knelt at her feet. He touched her inner thigh with the tip of his finger.

"I like seeing you wet with my come. Although I would prefer it if my seed was buried deep inside you busy creating a child. If I had my way, you'd be chained to my bed and wet like this all the time." He leaned forward, kissed her flesh, licked his way up to her clit. "I'd leave you like this in the morning, have you all day and by the evening you'd be covered in my seed and still wanting more." He caught her around the back of the knees as she staggered against him and lifted her into his arms.

"What a shame that we live in such civilized times and that you no longer want me."

# Chapter Five

## ಕ

God, she was so frustrated. Douglass slid out of bed and walked across to the window. A week had passed since her last conversation with Marcus and true to his word, he hadn't tried to have sex with her. The trouble was, he hadn't stopped Sven, Harlan and Bron from visiting her every day and priming her for his lovemaking either.

She glared at the bed where Bron still slept, his face hidden in the tangled sheets. Endless foreplay was not enough. She wanted a real man between her thighs, a real cock thrusting deep into her sheath making her come again and again. Correction, she wanted Marcus. With a stifled sound she hugged herself. There was no way she was going to beg him to make love to her.

To her surprise, she found she missed his presence in other ways. Despite the lack of lovemaking, he spent plenty of time with her. From the many conversations they shared she'd discovered he was an intelligent, thoughtful man who obviously cared deeply about the welfare of his people. Okay, he had a massive blind spot about women, but she could even understand that if she tried really hard.

She stared at the two moons which hung over the distant Purple Desert. Perhaps it would be better for everyone if she stayed at the spaceport until the rescue ship arrived. She obviously wasn't meant for a life of pure sexual indulgence. She only wanted one man. A man capable of being not only a father to Danny, but her best friend and a fantastic lover. She sighed. Not that she wanted much. Bron snorted in his sleep and burrowed even further under the covers. Somehow she didn't think Marcus would just let her leave. As quietly as she could, Douglass scooped up Bron's tunic and cloak and put them on. If things got rough and she had to make it to the port by herself, her first task was to find a way out of the palace.

It was dark on the lower levels, the lamps extinguished and the paths empty of people. The soft roar of the fountain echoed through the passageways. A hint of dew touched her skin. After a wary glance around, Douglass crept down the stone stairs, her bare feet made no sound. Marcus had said the kitchens, storage and guards rooms lay below the fountain level. Surely there would be an unguarded exit somewhere? She shivered as the stairwell narrowed and her fingers brushed cold, wet stone.

At the bottom of the steps, three passages led off into the darkness. Voices rose from both left and right. She sniffed the air and guessed from the savory smells that the kitchens lay to her right. Wishing she had thought to bring a lamp or candle, she decided to follow the central path. Blackness engulfed her and she had to put her hand out to touch the wall to guide her progress.

A sudden waft of fresh air assaulted her. Douglass gasped as she stumbled down into a larger cavern which seemed open to the night. Her eyes were blinded by the sudden light. When she got to her feet she found three men staring at her. All of them were tall and all of them looked delighted to see her. Fear curdled low in her belly. The cavern appeared to be full of food and barrels of ale.

She took a step backward. "I'm sorry, good sirs; I was looking for the kitchen."

The largest and ugliest of the men strolled toward her. His long black hair was matted and filthy. When he smiled, his teeth matched his hair.

"What's the hurry, little lady? We don't get to see many females down here, do we, lads?"

Douglass took another hasty step and her back hit the cave wall. "I must go. My family will be looking for me."

"I bet they will. A fine-looking female like you?" The man rubbed his crotch as he stared at her. "I'll wager there are a hundred men begging to rut between your thighs every night."

She didn't like the way his gaze fixed on her breasts. There was no sense of worship here, only a basic savage need. Before she could run, he grabbed her arm and brought it behind her back.

"Oh no, my pretty. Black Ivan just wants a look at you. Don't rush off."

She kicked his shins as hard as she could, pointless of course without shoes, as he fondled her breast with one dirty hand. The other two men crept closer. Lowering her head to her chest she brought it sharply up under Ivan's chin. His jaws snapped together with a satisfying crunch. He yelled in pain and slapped his hand over her mouth.

"She's a feisty little bitch, isn't she? I suggest we leave our cargo here and take the girl as our wages instead of the paltry sum of money the king's quartermaster gives us. We could charge every man who wanted to rut with her a gold piece." He squeezed her breast until she fought a scream. "I reckon she could service thirty men a night at least. We'd be rich in no time at all."

She closed her eyes at the rancid scent of Black Ivan's breath as he kissed the top of her head. Why hadn't she listened to Marcus? He'd warned her to stay upstairs. By ignoring his advice like some stupid heroine in a horror flick, she'd just signed her own death warrant.

"You will have to get through me if you wish to abduct my consort."

Douglass gasped as she was rotated back toward the entrance to the cave. Marcus stood there, his sword drawn, Sven and Bron behind him.

Black Ivan laughed. "And who might you be, the bloody king?"

"Aye, you have that right." Marcus moved closer, his sword leveled at Ivan's throat. "Give her up and I will allow you to leave."

His quiet tone seemed to unnerve her captor who loosened his grip on her mouth. Douglass sank her teeth into his palm and held on like a rabid dog as he tried to shake her loose. She lost her footing and fell to her knees, only then releasing her grip on her abductor's flesh. When she opened her eyes, Black Ivan was on the ground and Marcus stood over him.

Sven pulled her to her feet, his expression thunderous. He pointed at Bron and Harlan who had just arrived at the door. "Go with them until the king is ready to deal with you."

Normally she would have bristled at his tone but she was so glad to hear his voice that she obeyed him. Without a backward glance, she allowed Bron to lead her to the king's bedchamber. When both men retired to await the king outside the door, she sank to her knees and allowed the fear to overwhelm her.

When Marcus approached his bedchamber, Bron stopped him, his expression grave.

"I was at fault, Sire. I allowed your consort to leave the room whilst I slept." He swallowed hard and stood to attention. "If you decide I am unworthy to serve you, I will willingly step down from my position."

Marcus sighed. "Bron, my consort is not the easiest of people to guard. That is why I have a second man posted on the stairwell. I have been expecting her to try something like this." He patted Bron's shoulder. "If you learn from this mistake and continue to serve her well, I see no reason to demote you."

"Thank you, Sire." Bron's voice wobbled with relief.

With an encouraging nod, Marcus went into his bedchamber. The sight of Douglass going through his possessions revived all his anger. In an effort not to pick her up and shake her, he leaned back against the door.

"What exactly are you doing, my consort?"

She continued to throw the contents of his clothes chest onto the floor.

"I'm looking for some condoms or a vibrator." She raised her head and he saw the suggestion of tears in her eyes. "I realized that lack of sex was driving me crazy."

"I don't understand."

She stood up, one of his tunics fisted in her hand. "Yes, you do. I can see how much you want to yell at me, well, just go ahead. What I did was stupid and dumb and irresponsible, okay? And the only thing I can come up with, or say in my defense, is my current obsession with sex, or the lack of it."

His anger dimmed at her frank admission of guilt. "You misunderstand me, consort. That is not what confused me. I don't know what condoms or vibrators are." He risked a smile at her. "But I can easily appreciate that lacking me in your bed might drive you crazy."

"You are such a conceited...bastard." She threw his tunic at him. He caught it in one hand. It occurred to him that she challenged him in a way no other woman of his world ever would. Despite her short stature, every inch of her radiated defiance.

He dropped the tunic on the floor. "The solution to your problem is easy. Come to bed with me. I promise to keep you well pleasured until you have no thoughts of running away again."

She sighed. "I wasn't planning on leaving tonight. I just wanted to make sure I had an escape route if I needed one."

He unclasped his cloak and drew his tunic over his head. Her eyes widened as they fastened on his erection. He ran his fingers over his shaft and gently squeezed. "Ah, so tonight was more of a scouting expedition." For some reason, her words lessened the pain that had settled in his gut when he believed she intended to run.

"I didn't mean to cause all this fuss or put anyone's life in danger."

He held her gaze. "The only life in danger was your own. Perhaps you should pay for what you have done."

She raised her chin a notch. "Are you going to lock me in a dungeon and throw away the key?"

He walked toward her, blood pooling in his groin, desire warming his belly. Up close, he registered the depth of her reaction to the violence she had witnessed, the fine trembling of her limbs, the fear in her eyes. "I have a much better way to deal with you than that. What is that old Earth saying? 'Make the punishment fit the crime'?"

She swallowed hard as he halted in front of her. "I am truly sorry for behaving like an idiot but you have put me in a difficult position."

He touched her cheek, rubbed his thumb over her generous lower lip. "Your position is not difficult, consort. You are the one who makes it so." With one hand he captured her wrists in the small of her back. His cock brushed the fabric of her borrowed tunic. He drew the dagger tucked under the narrow leather strap at the top of his thigh and slit her tunic from top to bottom.

She shivered as the rough cloth fell away to reveal her breasts. His shaft rubbed against her belly, the crown almost between her breasts. Instinct shouted at him to reclaim her and calm her fears in the most basic way possible but he knew she wasn't ready to respond to him yet.

"If you will not accept my seed, perhaps I will pleasure myself instead."

He picked her up and dumped her in the center of his bed. As she struggled to right herself, he sat cross-legged, his back to the headboard. He placed his hands around her waist and drew her to sit across his knees facing him, her legs spread wide, giving him an intimate view of her pussy.

He waited until she regained her balance before he removed his hands. "Tell me what a condom is."

Douglass stared at him, her blue eyes wary. "Are you kidding me?"

He shrugged. "If by that do you mean am I joking, I am not. Why would this thing relieve your sexual tensions?"

"It's a form of protection against fertilization. A man sprays his penis with a fast-setting synthetic foam or uses a ready-made sheath to cover him completely so that when he ejaculates, the sperm cannot escape."

Marcus stroked his cock with one finger. "This foam works?"

Douglass watched the slow glide of his finger. "In most cases it does. Occasionally it might tear but that's rare these days."

"Why would a man not wish to fertilize his woman?"

"Because on Earth, some people have sex without staying together and making a family and other people have sex just for fun."

He concentrated on massaging his cock and tried to imagine it encased in plastic. He shuddered at the thought. "But sex has a deeper meaning than mere pleasure. It ensures the procreation of the species. It is in everyone's best interest if a couple stays together to produce and rear a child."

Douglass sighed deeply, her breasts trembled in time making him want to suckle them. "I'm not sure if anyone thinks about that anymore and sometimes it's simply too painful for a couple to stay together. Although I'm somewhat inclined to agree with you."

He wrapped his fingers around his shaft and slowly pumped. The slick, wet slide of his pre-come sounded loud in the silence. Douglass licked her lips.

"For me, there is nothing as exciting as the feel of your body yielding to my cock as I first push inside you." He glanced up at her. "If a man wears one of these condoms, surely he cannot feel the tightness of a woman's sheath as it grips him?"

"I've heard men complain about that."

Marcus allowed himself a small smile at the breathiness of her reply. She seemed unable to take her eyes away from his still growing rod. "Have you noticed any difference between the feel of my cock and that of a man with a condom?" He encircled his shaft with finger and thumb. "Although, I am reputed to be large, so perhaps there is no comparison."

She gave a shaky laugh. "You are the biggest man I've ever seen." Her gaze flicked down to her pussy. "I'm amazed that you fit in there at all." Droplets of her cream slid down her parted thighs and made her curls glisten. He longed to thrust his fingers deep inside her to gauge how wet and ready she was for him. "And yes, it does feel different."

He held her gaze. "Better or worse?"

"Better without the condom."

He smiled and continued to work his shaft. Enjoying the slow buildup of passion and Douglass watching him. "And what was the other thing you spoke of?"

"A vibrator?"

He lifted his soaked fingers to her mouth and spread his seed on her lips. "Is that like a condom?"

"No, it's," she hesitated as she bit her lip and tasted him. "It's kind of a mechanical cock."

He stopped moving his fingers. "Why would any woman need something like that?"

She wriggled restlessly against his thighs. "Because men on Earth are not the greatest lovers and if a woman wants to feel sexually satisfied sometimes she has to take care of it herself." She shook her head. "I can't believe I'm having this conversation. I feel like the oldest whore in a brothel breaking in a virgin."

Laughter shook through him at her exasperated expression. "I am no virgin. This vibrator, is it shaped like a real cock?"

"Usually, although most of them are bigger than the average man."

He gripped his shaft. "Bigger than me?"

"No."

"Good." He continued to touch himself, slid a hand under his aching balls and gently fingered them. "I can see why women might desire a man as big as me, but surely there is no comparison to a real man thrusting inside a woman?"

"No."

Her answers had become shorter and shorter. He studied her beneath lowered lashes. She was definitely more relaxed, No hint of fear haunted her eyes. "You seem quiet. Do you not like your punishment, consort?"

Her gaze snapped back to his face. "This is my punishment?"

"Aye, do you not remember? Making the punishment fit the crime. It drove me wild seeing you in that man's hands. Now I'm going to drive you wild and there is nothing you can do about it either."

Her eyes flashed a challenge and she darted closer and licked the crown of his cock. "Perhaps I'll drive you wild first."

"I'm counting on it, consort."

He pushed her gently onto her knees. Slowly he removed the very long supple strap of leather he wore wrapped around his thighs and groin. He bound her wrists behind her back and brought the rest of the strap between her legs. He arranged it carefully over her clit. The rest he brought up between her breasts and around her neck.

"I can't touch your pussy now, even if I want to, so you can suck my cock all you want."

When she leaned forward, the leather strap loosened. He wound the remainder of it around his wrist, tightening it against her flesh. She gasped as he pushed his cock between her lips. She sucked hard. He slid one hand in her long black hair to keep her exactly where he wanted her.

Her hands fisted behind her back as he flexed the leather back and forth. His balls tightened unbearably as she continued to suck him deep down her throat. As he fought for breath he realized that she was shuddering and crying out, climaxing without him laying a finger on her. With a roar, he exploded into her mouth, felt his come cascade in thick, flowing waves down her throat, wished he was buried deep in her sex.

He unwrapped the leather and released her hands. To his surprise she seemed content to simply lie in his arms, her breathing ragged, and her body still shaking with the aftereffects of her orgasm. Sleep pricked at his eyes and he allowed it to rise over him. For the first time in his life he had a woman in his bed who refused to have sex with him. Yet he felt as relaxed and fulfilled as a man who had experienced a hundred couplings.

In his desperate desire for a child, he'd forgotten that, alongside their physical passion, his parents had liked and respected each other. Like a prize bull, he'd begun to see females as something to fertilize rather than as potential life mates. Douglass had changed all that. His desire to sleep deserted him as he stroked her hair. What spell had this challenging slip of a woman cast over him and why was he content just to hold her in his arms?

\* \* \* \* \*

In the massive palace stable yard, Douglass approached the creature warily from one side. Despite her initial concern, it seemed to be dozing in the bright sunlight. Its overall shape, especially the long nose and sharp teeth, reminded her of a dragon but it was covered in silky green feathers. She glanced up at Marcus who was grinning at her.

"What exactly is it?"

"It's a *wulfrun*." He raised an eyebrow. "Don't you have them on Earth?"

The beast shifted on its clawed feet and sighed, blowing hot fetid air in Douglass' face.

She took a hasty step back. "No, unfortunately, we don't. It looks like something from a fairy tale or a legend."

Marcus reached forward and patted the animal's neck. "They are quite safe. We use them for all our transport needs." He nodded to one of the stable hands who threw a blanket over the *wulfrun*'s back and strapped on a bridle. A second animal was brought forward and tied up beside the first.

"I thought you wanted to get out of the palace, consort?" Marcus mounted the larger of the two *wulfruns* and sat looking down at her. "Are you too afraid to risk your skin?"

Douglass held his challenging stare as she approached the *wulfrun*. With Sven's help, she managed to clamber onto the back of the creature. She gripped the reins before giving Marcus a triumphant smile. Beneath her butt, the coiled muscles of the animal shifted.

"I'm not scared, Sire. I enjoy a good ride."

Marcus winked at her. "I know that, consort." He clicked his teeth and headed for the archway which led out of the high-walled stable yard. Letting out a deep breath, Douglass squeezed her legs against the *wulfrun*'s soft sides and tightened her left rein.

To her surprise, the *wulfrun*'s gait was similar to a horse. She quickly adjusted to the smooth rhythm of the creature's long stride and caught up with Marcus. For the first time in over two months she had the opportunity to look around her. To her annoyance, the eight men spread out around her and the king kept her from seeing much more than she had inside the palace.

"Are all these men necessary?" Douglass gestured at their escort.

Marcus looked surprised. "It's only my bodyguard."

"But I can't see anything. They are blocking my view."

"That's the general idea. They are here to protect you."

Douglass brought the *wulfrun* to a halt. "I thought you said they were your bodyguards, not mine."

Marcus stopped as well. "They are sworn to protect what is mine, consort."

"I'm not your possession. I can protect myself."

His expression tightened. "As I've already told you, women are scarce on this planet. After your recent experiences you should know that some men would do anything to find and keep a fertile woman for their tribe."

Douglass started moving again, her temper rising. "If you taught your women to fight, they wouldn't need to be protected. They could protect themselves."

"But why should they have to? Women are meant to be loved, cherished and honored for their ability to bear children. Why should they have to fight when men can do it so much better?"

"Because they are not children or possessions," Douglass snapped. "They are adults who should be free to make choices for themselves."

Marcus stared at her, his lips compressed in a thin line. Without another word, he dug his heels into the sides of his *wulfrun* and galloped toward the brow of the hill. After a short struggle with her temper and her conscience, Douglass followed him. He waited for her, his bodyguard spread out around him like a cloak.

Below them lay lush orchards of fruit trees and fields of golden crops. Douglass breathed in the scent of pollen and the thick cloying essence of living things. In the distance the curved purple hills of the desert surrounded the valley floor like arms around a child. Marcus stared straight in front of him.

Douglass cleared her throat. "I should not have criticized your customs, Sire. One of the most important rules they taught us in Space Academy was not to try and understand another planet's social system and culture after a five-minute visit."

Marcus swung around to look at her. "When she was fifteen, my sister was abducted by a band of men from one of the outlying villages."

Douglass gulped.

"We were staying in our summer residence far in the north. By the time my father and I found her again she'd been forced to endure several pregnancies. She died in my arms trying to birth her fifth child at the age of twenty." His smile was shadowed with grief. "So you see, even the protection I offer you might not be enough."

The bitterness in his voice made her reach out and touch his arm. "I can only repeat my apology. As I said, I have no right to criticize."

Marcus laid his hand over hers. "Perhaps, one day when the birthrate increases and women become plentiful again they will be able to be as fearless as you."

Douglass didn't know what to say. It was obvious Marcus was no woman-hater. He truly believed that women were safer kept in seclusion. And perhaps, because of his personal experiences and the current situation on his planet he had a point.

"Are your women allowed to learn to read and write?"

Marcus looked insulted. "Of course they are."

"So the only thing they are not allowed to do is work outside the home?

"It depends on the community they live in. Some women are well protected and are able to work in the fields or alongside their men." Marcus leaned forward and persuaded his *wulfrun* to move down the slope of the hill. Douglass followed him.

"If a woman wanted to get a job like mine, would she be able to?"

Marcus smiled at her. "I'm not exactly sure what you do, consort."

Douglass gave him a mock salute. "I deliver parcels throughout our galaxy for the United Planetary Parcel Service, the UPPS."

"Ah, and that is an important job?"

"I suppose it depends on whether you need a package delivered urgently. With such a small space ship, I'm fast and efficient."

"It is more important to you to have this job than to breed children?"

"I can do both. On Earth, women are free to have both a career and a family."

Marcus grunted. "It is an interesting concept, but one my own people would find hard to understand."

Douglass flicked him a glance as they reached the first of the fruit trees. "Do I seem unfeminine to you then? Does having a job make me less of a woman in your eyes?"

He studied her for a long slow heartbeat. "That is the most interesting thing of all, my consort. You are the most fascinating woman I have ever met."

With a flourish he dismounted and helped Douglass down, his hands firm around her waist. He continued to stare at her as if she were a very interesting puzzle. She could only be glad that he hadn't taken her outspoken opinions the wrong way. His ability to listen only increased her admiration for the quiet intelligence and strength she believed lay behind his impressive physical appearance.

Was he learning to appreciate her as a person and see beyond her baby-making capacities? She began to hope he was. He was certainly the most remarkable man she'd met in a long while.

"Would you care to stroll in the orchard out of the heat?" Marcus guided her into the shade of the wide canopied trees. She laid her hand on his arm.

"I think that would be delightful."

Something flew past her head and hit the king right in the chest. She gasped as he pushed her behind him and drew his sword. The bodyguards spread out, shouting to each other as they pursued a small shape that flitted between the trees.

"I have him, Sire!"

Douglass let out her breath as Sven emerged, grinning, holding the culprit by the scruff of his neck. Marcus started to laugh as he wiped splashes of overripe *ozan* fruit from his face. He let go of Douglass and went down on one knee in front of the young fruit thrower.

"That was a very good shot. What is your name?"

She guessed the boy was about the same age as Danny and obviously just as mischievous. He was the first child she'd seen since her arrival on the planet.

"My name is Erik." He glanced back at Sven and scowled. "Are you going to tell on me?"

"Of course not. No damage was done. "Marcus said.

Douglass glanced to her left as a woman emerged from the trees, her yellow head covering flapped in the wind. From her stricken expression, Douglass guessed she had a good idea what her son had been up to. The woman fell to her knees beside Erik and drew him into her arms. Erik immediately tried to wiggle free.

"Please, my King. He meant no harm. He is just a boy."

Marcus reached forward and touched Erik's thick brown hair, his fingers lingered. His gentleness no longer surprised Douglass. She allowed herself to imagine how Marcus would deal with Danny when he misbehaved.

"I was just congratulating your son on his excellent marksmanship." Marcus got to his feet, bringing the woman with him. "You must bring him to the palace when he is older to watch my warriors train. Perhaps he might win a place among them."

Erik's face glowed with excitement as he faced the king. "I would like that. Can we go tomorrow, Mama, please?"

Marcus patted his head. "Your mother will decide when you are old enough, so don't pester her or she might change her mind."

The mild threat was enough to make Erik stop talking although he couldn't quite stop jumping up and down. His mother wrapped her arms around him. With a sharp pang of longing, Douglass wished she could hold Danny like that. Inhale the intriguing scent of little boy before he grew tired of the caress and fidgeted to be set free.

Leaving Marcus to talk to the young woman, she walked back toward the *wulfrun*. She no longer saw the beauty of the valley around her. How long would it be before Danny forgot her and turned to another woman for the comfort only a mother could give? She rebuked herself for the self-pitying thought. She and Danny had always been close, sharing secrets and laughter as easily as they shared milk and cookies.

One of the *wulfruns* nuzzled her hair and she patted its nose. Whatever the risks, Danny needed her and would expect her to get home to him. She would simply have to find a way.

# Chapter Six

## ಏ

Douglass stared out of the window and strained to imagine the darkness of space beyond the purple-tinged planetary atmosphere. The sun hadn't risen yet and the palace was shrouded in shadows. She wiped a tear from her cheek. Dreams of her son had woken her from an uneasy sleep. Had Danny realized that she should've been back by now? Had her mother had to endure the UPPS officials arriving at the door to tell her that her daughter was missing?

"Why are you crying, consort?"

She shivered as Marcus placed his hands on her shoulders.

"I was thinking about my family on Earth."

He kissed the top of her head. "And missing them, no doubt." He sighed, his breath warm against her skin. "I will talk to the engineer at the spaceport again tomorrow and see if we can increase our signal strength and make contact with your people."

"I still don't understand why they haven't responded to my ship's emergency calls."

He shifted her back until he could wrap his arms around her. "It's possible that if our planet isn't on their charts, they simply haven't realized exactly where you are yet. I'm sure they will find you."

She leaned back against his chest, surprisingly grateful for his presence. "Then there's nothing I can do but wait, is there?"

He chuckled, the sound resonating deep in his chest. "You could try and enjoy what I offer you, consort." He nipped her ear until she squirmed against him.

"But it feels wrong to enjoy myself when my family is probably worried sick."

He turned her to face him, his expression serious. "But you have already admitted there is nothing else you can do."

She tried to smile. "But I still feel guilty."

His face softened. "My mother always said women were born feeling guilty. When she refused to put herself first, my father would take her away into the mountains for a few days and devote himself to her sexual pleasure. She always came back in a more relaxed frame of mind."

Douglass touched the dimple on his chin. He was right; she wasn't used to thinking about her own needs and desires. Since Danny's birth, she'd forgotten how to be a woman and concentrated only on being a mother and a provider. Could she allow herself to enjoy Marcus' sexual attention and not feel any guilt? The very idea of it made her body heat with desire. She studied his face. His affection for his parents always surprised her. She sensed he would cherish his own family even more.

"So you think I should relax and enjoy myself then?"

He kissed her cheek and drew her into a close embrace. "I know that this is hard for you, but what can't be changed must be endured. Isn't it better for you to be here safe in my arms rather than dead in the desert or captured by a tribe of men who expect you to service them all until you die from it?"

She shuddered, remembering the rough feel of Black Ivan's hands on her. "I hadn't thought of it like that. I suppose I should be grateful to be alive."

Marcus picked her up in his arms and headed back to the bed where Sven lay sleeping. "That's an excellent way to think, consort. Now all you have to do is beg for my cock and I too will be happy."

She stifled a laugh as he dropped her onto the bed and eyed his enormous erection. "That's going a bit too fast for me."

He bent forward and kissed her carefully on the mouth, his wet cock nudged her breasts. "Then I too will be patient and wait for my heart's desire."

She closed her eyes as he lay down next to her and held her tight. His understanding and compassion undermined her. Suddenly, it seemed cruel that achieving her desire to go home meant that Marcus would never achieve his.

Later that morning, Marcus and his men had streamed out of the palace toward the purple deserts on their daily hunting expeditions. She scowled at the thought. She could have gone with them. She'd already shown she could ride a *wulfrun*.

Another slow week had passed since her last outing and he had done nothing to ease her captivity since. Douglass gazed around her beautiful suite. Harlan strummed a lute in the corner, the melody soothing, his voice matching perfectly. She was well fed, well taken care of. Any sexual desire she expressed to her servers was eagerly satisfied. What right did she have to feel so trapped?

She wasn't stupid. She already knew that riding off by herself into unknown territory would risk not only her own life but the lives of those who protected her. But it was still as frustrating as hell.

Douglass shot to her feet. "Where are Bron and Sven?"

Harlan put down the lute. "They are practicing their weaponry skills in the indoor arena."

Douglass looked around for something to cover her nakedness. "Great. I'm going to watch them."

Harlan held out his hand in a placating gesture. "Consort, I don't think the king would want you to witness such bloodthirsty activities."

"The king's never seen me watching a Raiders football game either."

Douglass headed for the door wrapped securely in one of the silk sheets from her bed. "Don't worry if you don't wish to come with me, Harlan," she said airily, "I'll find it myself. I believe Marcus said it was on the same level as the sculpture of his parents."

Harlan strapped on his sword and dagger and ran after her. "I'll take you, my lady, but I still don't think the king will be pleased."

Douglass tried to enter the arena quietly but the massive door slipped through her fingers and crashed back into the wall. Sven and Bron stopped mid-fight and looked up. She waved at them.

"Carry on; just pretend I'm not here."

Both men were coated in a fine sheen of sweat. Narrow leather straps protected their groins and tops of their thighs. It was a pleasure to sit and watch their graceful yet lethal movements. Douglass could only admire Sven's skill and patience as he led Bron through a series of complex maneuvers seemingly designed to behead an enemy with two swords.

Eventually, Sven tossed his swords to Bron and advanced on Douglass. "This is not a fit place for you, my lady."

She glared at him. "Why not? I can fight."

Sven failed to stifle a grin. "You? Why would a woman as beautiful as you ever need to fight?"

Douglass grabbed Harlan's dagger, let the sheet unravel and started hacking through the swaths of silk. When she'd constructed a simple, short tunic length, she ripped a final hole in the center and put her head through it. Another narrow strip cut from the sheet worked as a belt around her waist.

Harlan retrieved his dagger and stepped smartly out of the way as Douglass marched down the steps to confront Sven. She poked him in the chest with her index finger.

"I can fight, pal. Where I come from, it pays to be able to defend yourself."

After her dismal performance against the men she'd encountered in the caves beneath the palace, she felt a desperate need to prove herself.

Sven picked her up and dumped her in the arena sand. He swaggered three steps back and spread his arms wide. "Come then, my bloodthirsty wench. Attack me."

Douglass dropped into a crouch and circled him. It was one of her greatest pleasures in life, cutting a big smug man down to size. Martial arts training made no concessions to size, only ability, and she had plenty of that. She came in close, pivoted back onto her right leg and kicked out with her left, catching Sven in the ribs. His grunt of surprise and sudden move to catch her foot made Douglass smile.

She stepped out of range and eyed her target again. He often complained of an old knee injury. Now which knee was it? To her delight, this time, Sven wasn't content to stand there grinning. He rushed her, one hand out in front of him. She dodged to the side and caught his right knee with three swift kicks. When he staggered, she followed up with another blow to his thigh and an elbow in his throat.

Sand rose in a thickening cloud as he fell onto his back. Douglass leapt onto his chest and grabbed his balls in her fist. Sven froze.

"Are you ready to take back your words?" She smiled at Sven's belligerent expression. She tightened her grip. He stifled a groan.

"All right, consort, you fight well. Now will you release me?"

Douglass continued to squeeze his cock until he grew hard and wet. His hips thrust forward into her hand. "All's fair in love and war, Sven. Didn't you know that?"

With a roar, he rose up and caught Douglass around the waist. "I can think of another game you might like to play, my lady." He pulled off her sash and wrapped it around her eyes. "Let's see how good you are with your eyes covered."

He pulled her to her feet and spun her around. When she stopped, Douglass put out her hand and felt nothing. She concentrated on controlling her breathing and reacting to the subtle movements around her. A rush of air signaled the sound of ripping silk, leaving her naked. Fingers tweaked her nipple. She lashed out with her foot but connected with nothing but air. A slap on her butt sent her spinning to her left. She collided with a man's chest and guessed from the accompanying grunt that she'd hit Sven again.

After an endless session where her body was touched, aroused, tormented and stimulated, she was panting, half with desire and half with fatigue. A cold rush of air warned her that someone else had entered the arena. A strong arm looped around her waist and held her close. Sven's distinct pine scent warmed her nostrils. He plunged his fingers inside her until she writhed against his stomach.

"The king has brought you a gift." Sven rubbed her clit with his thumb and then spread her juices back toward her anus. "He wants to penetrate you here as well." His finger slid past her tight anal bud. "But he fears you are too small to take him."

He turned her around until her breasts were crushed against his hard chest; he spread his fingers over her butt, one long finger settling between her cheeks. Douglass stiffened as something much thicker than a finger thrust inside her. Whatever it was, it was cold and smooth like glass. She moaned as Sven slid all four fingers into her pussy.

"She likes it, my King."

Douglass jumped as another hand caressed her heated butt. All the slaps and fondling had heated her skin, sending her nerve endings crazy. She inhaled the scent of Marcus' arousal, as familiar to her now as her own.

His fingers probed the glass plug. "I'm bigger than this. Do we have anything larger?"

"Harlan, Bron, hold her."

Douglass was lowered to her knees as Sven disappeared. She strained her ears to hear him, distracted as Marcus gently stroked her clit and pushed the plug farther inside her. Harlan's breathing sounded harsh as he brought her nipples to hard rigid points.

"This is bigger, my lord," Sven said. "I have some scented oil here to ease the way."

Douglass held her breath as the first glass plug was removed. The spicy scented oil with a hint of citrus felt cold against her heated skin as Marcus massaged it into her and slid his fingers past her anus.

"Let out your breath, my consort. Take the plug deep inside."

Sven's finger stroked her oil-soaked sex as Marcus slid the new glass plug home. Douglass panted as she struggled to accept the width and depth of the rod. A murmur of deep male satisfaction spread around her. She could tell they were all aroused. She wondered how she looked to them, legs wide open, butt thrust upward, her pussy wet and swollen, her anus clenching around a huge glass object.

Even as she had the thought she came, her pussy clenching around nothing until Marcus pumped four fingers inside her. Bron and Harlan came with her and she felt their come dripping down either side of her hips. Marcus guided her head to Sven's cock.

"Take him in your mouth, consort. Let me watch."

She closed her mouth around Sven and sucked hard as Marcus worked more of the glass plug inside her. Sven came with a roar and Marcus slid the last inch of the plug home. He took Douglass by the hand and helped her to her feet. His hand splayed over her butt, keeping the plug inside her.

"We'll finish this in private."

Douglass remained blindfolded as he led her down a series of walkways. She sensed people watching them. Their king, naked and erect, his consort, covered in other men's come. Cool air and the sound of rushing water alerted her to a change in the place. She realized they were moving down. Was this one of the secret underground caverns Marcus had mentioned?

He guided her forward until her knees bumped into a stone wall. Grasping her around the waist, he picked her up and made her kneel on a smooth stone surface. Her hands were raised above her head and manacled together. Soft leather straps around her bent knees kept her thighs wide apart.

She blinked as Marcus finally removed the blindfold. They were in the remains of what appeared to be an ancient temple. A soft waterfall played against one sheer wall of black rock, gleaming in the soft light. Steam hissed from the rear of the cave hinting at heated bathing pools beyond.

Marcus knelt in front of her, his gaze fixed on hers. "In ancient times, this is where a consort waited for her king. On the days she was fertile she would be left like this. It was the duty of the temple maidens to keep her aroused and eager for her mate. When the king came to visit her, she was always available to him."

Douglass found her voice. "And I thought I had it bad being trapped in a luxurious suite with three men to pleasure me."

Marcus smiled, his oiled muscles rippled in the candlelight. His huge erection almost reached his navel. "Tonight, there is only me. I intend to pleasure you until you scream so much you lose your voice or until I run out of come." He looked down at his cock, smoothed a hand over its slick wetness.

Douglass felt a trickle of cream slide down her thigh. Marcus leaned forward and licked it, his tongue rough on the soft skin of her inner thigh. "Imagine how it must have felt, waiting here, waiting to be fucked, so aroused that the thought of your king's cock was all you could think about or desire."

As he spoke, Marcus opened a drawer concealed in the smooth marble and began taking out the contents. He squeezed oil on his fingertips and gently touched her nipples. "I want to make you mindless. I want you to give yourself up to my control completely."

"Is this because I disobeyed you and left my suite?"

He chuckled. "Nay, although I will punish you for that too if you wish."

She lifted her head to glare at him, saw the mixture of lust and amusement in his eyes and relaxed. He ran his finger over her lower lip and sighed.

"Consort, if you keep your promise not to go outside, I will allow you to train with your servers. I should have taken care of the matter sooner."

Douglass studied him through half-closed eyes as he leisurely coated her nipples in scented oil. His concern for her seemed genuine. How did he know she had more to give? She had to leave this planet and return to her old life and her child. How would she feel if she gave him everything? Relieved that she'd allowed a man to possess her completely for once in her life or horrified by her lack of control? Would she yearn to be back with him or be glad to have escaped?

A moan escaped her as Marcus oiled her clit and labia. She tried to push her hips forward to increase the pressure of his finger but her bonds held her rigidly in position. She could only take what he gave her, only receive what he wanted her to have and when he wanted her to have it. He spread her swollen pussy lips, fingering them between his thumb and forefinger. She'd almost forgotten the glass plug in her anus. He touched it now, pushing it firmly back into place.

"As you have no attendants except me, I'll have to arouse you first."

Douglass stared at him. "I am aroused. You know I am."

He smiled, his finger tracing her dripping sex. "Not enough. Remember, I want you thinking about one thing and one thing only. My cock. You're not ready for that yet. I want you to take me inside you. I want you to beg for me."

He stood up and kissed her, his mouth unhurried, his tongue slowly lapping at hers as if he had all the time in the world. She concentrated on the textures and scent of his lips, the thrust of his tongue against her own. His fingers closed over her nipples and tugged in rhythm to his kisses, harder and harder until they stood out from her breasts.

Douglass bit her lip as he attached clamps to her extended nipples and several chains to connect them together. He returned to tantalize her mouth, still slow and careful, not giving her enough, never giving her enough. Her chained nipples grazed his muscled chest with every subtle caress. She felt every hair on his chest as it brushed her flesh, his cock slid against her stomach, wet and hot.

She groaned when he drew back and studied her. Her pussy throbbed, reacting to the hardness of the butt plug deep inside her. He circled her and drew the hair away from the back of her neck. She shuddered as he bit lightly on the curve between her neck and her shoulder.

"Are you thinking about my cock?"

She tensed as the tip of his shaft pressed against the butt plug.

"Yes, of course I am."

He laughed, the sound caressing the back of her neck. "Not enough though. You're still thinking too hard. I want your mind to submit to me as well as your body."

"Why?"

He slid a hand around and cupped her mound. "Because you are my consort and I am your king. You owe me your obedience."

"I'm not one of your subjects. I have a life on another planet. I have a family."

Abruptly he removed his hand and walked around to face her. "You have a man who makes you as wet as I can? You have a man whose seed you want?"

He held out his hand palm up, showing her the thick pool of her cream. Holding her gaze he slowly bent his head and lapped it into his mouth.

"No. No one has ever made me feel like you do." Douglass hated herself for the admission but it was the truth. Why should she pretend otherwise? Even if she never saw him again, she'd always remember how he'd driven her wild.

He held her gaze, his golden eyes steady on hers. "Then perhaps you should enjoy me then and let me take control."

She stared right back at him. Her whole body quivering with need. With a sigh, she relaxed into the restraints, opening herself wider to him, ready to submit to his desires.

Marcus fell to his knees and rubbed his cheek against her stomach before heading down to her pussy. He breathed in and then flicked her clit with his tongue. She jumped as if he'd hit a nerve.

"Mmm…" he breathed. "Ready for a clamp, I think." She watched as he attached a thin gold loop to her clit and two clamps to her pussy lips. His fingers moved gently over her, exposing her secrets, displaying her for his sexual gratification. Douglass didn't care. She even liked it.

He looked up at her, his gaze narrowed. "I've often wondered how my ancestors got through their duties when they knew that their consort would be waiting for them like this." He caressed his shaft and balls and shuddered. "My cock ring feels too tight already. Imagine having to deal with the problems of your kingdom with a hard-on and your mind on fucking your woman."

He reached into the drawer again and extracted a large leather dildo. Douglass swallowed as he rubbed it against his dripping cock, coating it in his pre-come. "This is for you as well. It's not quite a vibrator but it serves a similar purpose. Watch me put it in."

The dildo slid inside her with ease, she was so wet. She fought the clenching on her internal muscles but couldn't stop herself coming. Her body arched against her restraints as her climax throbbed through her. Marcus watched her, one hand wrapped around his cock as she shuddered and moaned.

When she'd quieted, he stepped forward, slid his fingers into her hair and kissed her hard. "Next time you do that, I want to be inside you. Is that what you want?"

She couldn't reply, too caught up in a rising sensual haze to formulate a comprehensible answer. He replaced her blindfold. "Keep thinking about my cock. Decide whether you want to take my seed." He hesitated, his breath warm on her cheek. "Of course, if this is enough stimulation for you, I will not force myself on you."

He kissed the top of her head. "If you wish to mull over the true risk of giving yourself to me, consider this. By refusing me you deny us both a great deal of pleasure, and in truth, as I seem incapable of having children, perhaps your fears of becoming pregnant are unjustified."

His footsteps echoed in the high cavern as he retreated until she could no longer hear them. Had he gone to bathe in the steaming caverns she imagined lay beyond the temple? She pictured him lying back in the water, soaping his cock, thinking of her. Deprived of her sight, she could only concentrate on her body. Carefully she flexed her muscles. The softness of the leather and the hardness of the smooth glass complemented each other. Her womb throbbed, desperate for completion.

As time passed, she began to understand what Marcus wanted of her. With her body primed for his pleasure and her sight removed, she could only think of gaining her release. She also knew Marcus was the only man who could give her what she wanted. Would he take her slowly, drawing out each pleasure until it bordered on pain or would he be fast and hard and overwhelming?

By reminding her of his childless state, something she knew he must find difficult to even say out loud, he forced her to decide whether her fear of pregnancy was too great to enjoy his spectacular lovemaking. What did she want? She slowly let out her breath.

She wanted all of him. His lovemaking, his humor, the way he made her feel like the most valuable thing in his world. He was a man she could grow to love. Was it worth taking the risk of loving him to the best of her ability when she was still unsure whether he was capable of doing the same? Was it worth risking the possibility of carrying his child? She sensed he would be more than willing to accept Danny in his life. He would be no absentee father. If Marcus held true to his beliefs their child would be treasured and loved from the moment he knew it existed. For the first time in her life could she find a way to have everything she wanted?

Her world narrowed to the sensations coursing through her aroused body. Every breath she took tugged at the clamps on her nipples and reminded her of his mouth on them. Every twitch of a muscle brought her closer to orgasm and increased her sense of being stuffed full. She wanted his cock. She wanted to give him whatever he wanted.

She felt rather than heard him return. Her body tensed to instant awareness as the scent of his arousal reached her nostrils. She knew he stared at her. Did he like what he saw? Her body open, wet and ready for him? She let out a breath as he released her nipples from the clamps and then drew in another one as he methodically sucked her nipples in hard, pulsing strokes which went straight to her womb.

She came as he started on the second and he grunted his approval. His hands worked quickly on the other clamps as he continued to suckle her. She tensed as he moved behind her and took out the thick glass plug from her butt. Without speaking, he worked his cock inside her, spreading her butt cheeks wide as he pressed forward.

Douglass was glad for the support of the restraints as he thrust into her, his hands gripping her hips to hold her steady. She came again, muscles clenching against the leather dildo, wishing it was the flesh of his cock instead. He pulled out and she heard him washing himself.

He took her blindfold off and she winced against the sudden influx of light. He caught her chin in his fingers. "Tell me what you want."

"Your cock and your seed."

"Where?"

"Anywhere you choose to put it."

He didn't look away. "What if I took you out into the town square and fucked you there, would you let me?"

She stared right back at him. "Yes."

"What if I made you suck every man's cock in my bodyguard while I fucked you, would you let me?"

A tremor shook her at the thought of being on her hands and knees pleasuring other men while Marcus took his pleasure with her.

"Yes."

He removed the dildo, allowing her cream to pour out. "What if I wanted to fuck you until I ran out of come?"

"I am your consort. You are my King. I owe you my obedience in all things."

He circled her wrists with his hands. "Then take me and fuck me dry."

He surged into her on one strong heavy stroke, his hips pumping hard as he leaned into her. Douglass came after the first few thrusts and continued to climax as he kept up the even pace. His mouth descended possessively, demanding her submission, pushing her beyond pleasure into ecstasy. Her sheath milked him with a voracious strength that matched his cock.

She went beyond thinking, she only was. The circle of her awareness shrunk to what he was doing to her, how she couldn't direct his movements, how he had power over her. And yet, she sensed her own power even as she reveled in his, knew in her heart that she gave him what he demanded because she wanted to and not because she had no choice.

He roared as he finally came, the sound reverberating around the cavern as his hot seed pumped endlessly into her. He rested his forehead on her shoulder and drew her in a comforting embrace. Before he pulled out, he murmured, "That was just the beginning. Next I'm going to take you from behind and then, if you ask nicely, I might even let you go on top."

Dawn broke sending slivers of light through the palace walls as Marcus carried Douglass out of the cavern and up to his bedchamber. He held her close, felt her warm satisfied body relax in his arms. Oblivious to the people he passed, he concentrated on his consort's scent and the soft gleam of her long black hair.

An unaccustomed sense of protectiveness shook through him. By Thor's blood, if she gave him a child, he would be the happiest man in the universe. He would make her his queen and spend the rest of his days with her in his arms and in his life. His smile died as he laid her carefully on the huge bed. Why was he giving himself such false hope? He'd never sire a child. He'd never have a queen.

With an inarticulate sound, he buried his head in his hands. Was he destined to watch Douglass leave him as other women had when they discovered he couldn't give them a child? On his planet even his great wealth and power couldn't compensate for that loss.

She wasn't from his world. Could he persuade her to remain and simply be with him? He studied her sleeping form. She'd taken more than his seed during the last night. She'd taken his heart. Her courage and sensuality amazed and humbled him. Her permission to let him master her had forced him to acknowledge that he was her slave forever.

With a sigh and a prayer to the gods, he crawled into bed next to her and drew her into his arms. His cock stirred against the soft flesh of her belly. By Odin, he was sore. He resolutely shut his eyes and allowed sleep to overcome him.

# Chapter Seven

## ෨

"My King, you must get up!"

Douglass opened one eye to see Marcus sitting on the side of the bed as Sven strode into the room.

"What is the hurry, Sven?" Marcus stood and stretched giving Douglass a perfect view of his beautiful butt and muscled back.

"A delegation has arrived from the village of Hammersford. They insist you must see them at once."

"Hammersford? What in Thor's name do they want?" Marcus thrust a hand through his disordered hair and stared at Douglass. His slow smile left her staring at his mouth. "Perhaps they have some news about your ship, consort. We still haven't located the 'black box' you spoke of yet."

Douglass eased her aching body out of bed. Sven had already laid out her clothes besides Marcus'. She slipped on the silk tunic, wondering why she needed to be covered up and combed her hair while Sven helped Marcus dress more formally.

The great hall seemed strangely deserted when Marcus and Douglass reached it. Sunlight threaded down through the stained glass panels on the ceiling staining the stone floor in myriad overlapping colors. The small party from Hammersford was dwarfed by the magnificence of the cavernous space. Douglass took the seat Sven showed her to the right of Marcus' throne.

An elderly man took a hesitant step forward and bowed. "Sire? We bring you great news from our village."

Marcus inclined his head. "Welcome, Elder of Hammersford. We await your news with great interest."

Douglass stiffened as two women came to stand beside the elder. They were the first women she'd seen on the planet since her arrival. Both wore cloaks that concealed everything but their eyes. Marcus got slowly to his feet as one of the women fell to her knees.

"My King, I am Mistress Freya. I bring you a great gift." She gestured at the other woman. "Do you remember my daughter, Lillian? She was sent to your tent as tribute when you visited our village."

Marcus fisted his hands. "Uncover your face, Lillian. Let me see you."

Lillian removed her veil. Douglass thought she could barely be considered a woman. Her expression was a curious mixture of triumph and fear.

"Greeting, Sire. I bring you joyful news." She pulled her cloak away from her body and rested her hand on her stomach. "I carry your child. You will have an heir."

A roaring sound broke over the hall as Marcus' men responded to the announcement. Douglass felt the echo of it inside her head as well. Only one man stood as if unimpressed amidst the rejoicing.

Marcus held up his hand. "Perhaps we should discuss this matter in private." He gestured at his closest companions. "Accompany me to my chamber and summon my personal physicians."

Douglass allowed Sven to guide her from the hall. She knew she should feel happy for Marcus but somehow she couldn't. Something seemed off about the girl's announcement and Marcus' reaction to it. Would they allow her to sit in on the private meeting? Ignoring the stares of the people from Hammersford, she entered Marcus' private chamber as if she owned it.

The older woman who accompanied the girl tried to block her way. "Who is this woman, Sire? By what right does she enter your chamber?"

Marcus glanced at Douglass as she tried to outstare the other woman.

"Mistress Freya, Douglass is my acknowledged consort. She has a perfect right to be here."

"We'll see about that," Mistress Freya hissed as Douglass winked at her and sashayed past.


Marcus sat down and studied Lillian. "Are you sure the child is mine?"

Lillian didn't bother to hide the gleam of victory in her upturned gaze. "Of course, my King, I was a virgin when you bedded me. Who else could be the father but you?"

He stared into her eyes until she looked away. Beneath her delight all he could sense was the slick stink of terror. Had her family forced her into this position? He tried to remember the details of the night they had met. She'd drugged the wine she gave him and forced herself on him. He glanced around the small room at his attentive audience. If she truly carried his child, did he want to reveal such shameful details of their coupling? He wasn't worried about how he would be perceived; he was more concerned about the effect on his future child and its mother.

He tried to reform the scattered memories in his mind. Lillian's body gripping his cock, the pain of her fingernails digging into his biceps. He frowned at the thought. Had she even been a virgin? He had no recollection of it and no memory of any spilled blood. He looked up and caught

Douglass' interested gaze on him. By Thor. He loved her. How in hell was he going to explain this mess?

She gave him an encouraging wink. He straightened his spine.

"If it pleases you, Lillian. I will ask my physician to examine you before we make this news more widely known."

Sven grinned. "I should imagine it's too late for that, Sire."

Marcus bowed. "I still wish to make sure."

Mistress Freya put her arm around Lillian's shoulders. "Are you saying my daughter is lying?"

To Marcus' relief, his chief minister, Thorlan the Peacemaker, stepped forward, his calm face wearing a smile.

"Of course not, Lady Freya. The king meant no insult. You must understand that claims are made each year that the king has fathered a child. It is our duty as the king's Council to make sure that each particular claim is fully investigated."

Marcus waited until Lillian and her entourage was escorted from the room before he sat back in his chair. He should be feeling excited at the prospect of fatherhood. He'd dreamed of it all his life but the bitter taste in his mouth refused to leave. Why now when he believed he'd finally found a woman he could love?

Thorlan cleared his throat. "My King, you do not seem overjoyed by this news."

Marcus studied him. "Is it that obvious?"

"Do you deny having sex with this woman?"

"No. She was offered to me as tribute when I visited Hammersford." He noticed Douglass frown at his words.

She'd expressed her opinion of his planet's outdated views on women on more than one occasion.

"Then what is the problem?"

"The woman drugged my wine. She believed the rumors that I was incapable of performing and that I would kill her if she didn't conceive." His lip curled in self-disgust. "She gave me a powerful aphrodisiac to make sure I managed the job."

"But, excuse me, Sire, you penetrated her, yes? You left your seed in her?"

"I was so desperate for release I must have." Marcus couldn't bear to look at Douglass now. What would she think of the rumors that he was not only impotent but a mad despot who killed when he didn't get what he wanted?

Thorlan sat down with a thump, his robes swirling around him. "Are you suggesting she duped you in some way?"

Marcus rubbed at his eyes. "I don't know. She seemed too desperate for my liking. I tried to send her away but after the drug took hold of me, all I could think about was fucking."

A heavy silence unfolded over the room.

"If she was that desperate to have sex with you, perhaps she had something to hide."

Marcus looked up as Douglass spoke.

Thorlan intervened before Marcus could reply. "King's consort, your opinion is not required."

Douglass ignored Thorlan, her gaze fixed on Marcus. "Perhaps she—"

Thorlan stood up. "Sire, this woman is your lover. Anything she says could be biased. Of course she doesn't want to have her position usurped by your future queen and mother of your child."

Douglass got to her feet and marched toward Thorlan. She poked him in the chest with her finger. "Listen up, buster. I'm a woman, I know how women think. I'm perfectly capable of having a balanced opinion."

Thorlan kept talking. "With all due respect, you are an outsider. The Council is here to advise our king as to what is best for our planet. We cannot allow our personal preferences to influence a decision that might be vital for the future prosperity and very survival of our race. The hope of a child for the king would bring hope to everyone."

Marcus stood up. "He's right, consort. Perhaps we should allow my physician to examine Lillian first and determine whether she is with child or not."

"That's a great idea," Douglass said. "And if she is pregnant the DNA results will be able to confirm whether Marcus is the father or not."

"What is DNA?"

Douglass looked at Marcus for a long moment. "You don't have the technology to determine who the father of this child is?"

Marcus closed his eyes. "Obviously not." He glanced at his Council. "As I said, let's confirm the pregnancy first and take it from there."

Douglass waited until all the men, including Sven filed out. She crossed the room to Marcus' side.

"This woman, Lillian. Did you meet her before you met me?"

He wouldn't look at her. "Aye. I was leaving her village when I saw your craft crash into the desert. She was given to me as tribute. As king I have the right to procreate with any willing woman on the planet."

Douglass tried to smile even as pain stabbed behind her eyes. "How nice for you."

"Believe it or not, it becomes tedious after a while. I didn't want to touch Lillian. I wanted to send her away."

"Because she didn't please you?"

He groaned then, his head still in his hands. "Because I knew she didn't want me. I knew she'd been forced to offer herself to me by her village. By Thor, I'm almost old enough to be her father. I could see it in her eyes. She truly believed I would kill her if she didn't conceive."

Douglass put her hand on Marcus' knee. He gripped her fingers hard. "For the good of my planet, I have to believe that, however the child was conceived, the babe she carries is mine."

She recognized the desolation in his tone. She was right. He would make an excellent father. It echoed the sadness ringing through hers. She gathered her courage. "Do you want me to leave? I can go and stay at the hotel by the spaceport until my ride comes."

Marcus looked at her then, a faint smile on lips. "What ride would that be? So far we have received no response to our requests for help."

Douglass got to her feet and began to pace. "Perhaps we need to boost your signal. If I could return to the crash site and find the black box, I might be able to fire off another distress call."

She gasped as Marcus pulled her roughly into his arms.

"Nay, I don't want you to leave me. I need you."

She fought against the appeal of his hoarsely muttered words. He was a king. To admit his uncertainty and desire to her was a weakness. His mouth moved down her throat, kissing her with a savage intensity that made her knees give way.

"At least wait until my physician has confirmed the pregnancy. Then you can decide what you want to do next."

Douglass sensed his attempt to gather himself as if to negate his impassioned plea. She turned her head and kissed his cheek.

"I will stay for a little while." He drew back, his face composed once more. "Thank you."

\* \* \* \* \*

"I'm sorry, consort, but Mistress Freya has commandeered my services this morning." To his credit, Harlan didn't look thrilled at the prospect of leaving Douglass. "She wants me to assist Lady Lillian in her bath."

Douglass scowled at him. "But she's already borrowed Bron. Am I no longer allowed to see my own pleasure servants?"

Harlan bowed and headed for the door. Douglass got slowly off the bed and glanced at Sven who stood, arms folded, leaning against the wall. "Are you supposed to go and lick Lillian's precious feet too?"

Sven shook his head. "Nay, the king has asked me to stay with you."

Douglass waited until the door closed behind Harlan. "She is trying to undermine me, Sven."

"Who, consort?"

"You know damn well who. In the last four weeks since Lillian's pregnancy was confirmed, Mistress Freya has been determined to get rid of me."

Douglass moved restlessly to the window. In the courtyard below she saw Lillian, Marcus at her side, promenading in the vine-covered walkways. A wave of nausea curdled her stomach. Marcus looked attentive, his head bent toward Lillian as if he were interested in what she was saying.

A well of unaccustomed tears pricked at Douglass' eyelids. She'd promised Marcus she would stay, but things had changed. Lillian's pregnancy and Marcus' part in it made Douglass feel like an aberration, an embarrassment. She bit her lip as Lillian disappeared into the palace, headed for her bath and the tender ministrations of Harlan and Bron.

She shuddered as Sven came up behind her and put his hands on her shoulders. With a sigh, she leaned back against his solid chest. It was strange that the gruffest of her servers had become her closest ally.

"The king hardly visits me any longer. Does he visit Lillian's bed instead?"

Sven kissed the top of her head. "Consort, you know I cannot answer that. The king has the right to visit any bed he chooses."

She pushed away from him, hastily wiping at her face to conceal her tears. "Then perhaps I should find myself a different bed as well. I have a perfectly good one at home."

Sven held up his hand, a frown gathering on his face. "That is not a good idea. Speak to the king before you decide anything."

She glared at him as she pulled clothing out of one of the gilded chests. "He doesn't own me. I have a perfectly satisfactory life on another planet. I have a family. Perhaps I have simply outstayed my welcome."

With her head held high, she left the room, knowing that Sven would probably follow her but desperate to escape the stifling luxury of her empty suite. As she started down the stairs, she saw Marcus coming up them. With all the courage she could muster, she swept by his outstretched hand and ran as fast as she could.

He caught her by the stables and maneuvered her against the wall.

"Where do you think you are going? You are not supposed to come down here alone."

He looked tired, the lines of strain obliterating his forced attempt to smile.

"I am busy, my King. I have to arrange transport to the spaceport."

His eyes darkened and his grip on her arm increased. "You promised me you would wait."

"For what? You've obviously decided that Lillian is fit to be your queen and bear your child. Why should I wait around until she or her mother tosses me out on my ear or sends someone to poison me?"

"You are being ridiculous. I haven't decided anything."

Douglass gritted her teeth. "But you've allowed your Council to make the announcement for you. You've allowed Lillian to believe she is invincible."

"I had no choice. You do not understand."

"I understand all right. You chose what was best for your planet. Good for you." To her horror, her voice cracked and tears flowed down her cheeks.

Marcus tried to stop her tears with his fingertips, his expression appalled. "I didn't mean to do this to you. I am in hell. For the first time in my life my heart and soul are at war with my duty." He pressed his face against her throat and brushed her skin with his lips. She couldn't stop herself from touching his hair.

"Sire…"

Sven's warning came too late. Douglass looked up to find Lillian and her mother gaping at them from the end of the passageway.

Marcus straightened and moved away from her. "Is there something you wanted, Lady Lillian?"

Lillian smiled, her hand resting on her slightly swollen stomach. She pouted in Douglass' direction. "I thought you were coming to watch me bathe, Sire."

Douglass stared fixedly into the gloom of the stable wing. She couldn't bring herself to speak.

Sven bowed and stepped between her and Marcus, shielding her from the other women. "I will escort your consort to the stables, my King."

Dimly, Douglass heard Marcus' quiet reply before he moved away. She took a stumbling step forward. Sven caught her arm and steered her into a dark empty stall which smelled strongly of dung.

"Consort…" She walked into his arms and let him hold her until the storm of weeping subsided.


After her moment of weakness, Douglass found she was ready to fight again. She spoke to the king's stable master and found out about transport to the only spaceport. It seemed her options were limited to using one of the *wulfruns* or the more traditional female route of being taken in a closed litter carried by four men and surrounded by an armed guard.

The stable master was shocked that she even contemplated riding but she refused to let his disproval bother her. With Sven at her back she found very few of the men she encountered were prepared to argue with her.

On her way back to her suite, she turned to Sven who followed her at a discreet distance. He came up alongside her, one eyebrow raised.

"Do you think you could arrange for Mistress Freya to leave Lillian alone for a few minutes?"

Sven's broad face broke into a slow smile. "I can arrange that, consort." He winked at her. "Mistress Freya would be delighted to think that your personal server was interested in her instead."

Douglass kissed his cheek. "Thank you, Sven."

His voice was gruff as he stepped away. "The king is not happy. You make him happy, not the Lady Lillian."

To her delight, it took Sven very little time to spirit Mistress Freya out of Lillian's apartment. When she stepped through the ornate doorway, Douglass found herself in rooms very similar to her own. The silken drapes were closed tight, leaving the room in darkness. Lillian lay on the enormous bed eating the small yellow *ozan* fruit that grew in profusion in the palace orchards.

Her mouth formed a small O when she spotted Douglass. She struggled to sit up, her hands resting protectively over her belly. Her long thick brown hair fell to her waist like a child's.

"What do you want?"

The bowl of fruit fell to the floor. Douglass bent to pick it up and set it on the table.

"I don't want to frighten you. I just wondered if everything was all right."

Lillian's lip trembled. "Why should you care? You hate me. Everyone knows it."

"Who told you that?"

Lillian's lip stuck out even farther, making her look about five. "Everyone."

"Even the king?"

"Of course not. He won't talk about you even when Mother complains."

Douglass fought a smile. "I understand why your mother dislikes me but you and I should be friends. There are very few women here to talk to. And we have something in common. We both love the king."

Lillian's face crumbled. "I'm afraid of him." She gasped and covered her mouth, her eyes fearful. "Please don't tell my mother I said that...please."

"Why are you afraid of him?" Douglass edged closer until she could sit next to Lillian on the bed.

"Because he is the king."

"But you bear his child. You will be his queen."

Lillian looked away. "But I feel so ill. What if the babe is sick? What if it dies? He will kill me."

Up close, Douglass took another less jealous look at Lillian. Her stomach seemed swollen, her face was pale and her ankles bloated and misshapen. Douglass' antipathy fled and was replaced by a niggling concern. "Have you told the king's physicians how you feel?"

"They are like a bunch of frightened old women." Lillian sniffed. "If I tell them something is wrong, they will tell the king."

Douglass sought for patience as Lillian's expression became mulish. "He is a good man, Lillian. He would never hurt you."

Lillian's head drooped. Douglass studied her as the door to the chamber crashed open. One of Lillian's personal guards from Hammersford stood there. He glared at Douglass.

"Has she been upsetting you, Lillian? I...I mean, my lady?"

Douglass got up and walked toward him. "She was upset before I got here." She stared hard at the red-faced young man. "I'd say she's been upset for quite a while now." She turned to Lillian, who cowered in her bed, her brown eyes fixed on the guard. "If I were you, I'd talk to the king and tell him the truth."

Lillian shook her head, her eyes frantic, her attention still on the guard. "There's nothing to tell. I didn't say anything to her, Randall, I swear it. She is just making trouble."

The guard grabbed hold of Douglass' arm. "You do not understand how it is, you have no right to judge her."

Douglass shook her arm free. "I'm not judging her. I don't have that right, but if I cared for her happiness I might try and help her avoid a terrible mistake." She nodded at Lillian. "If you need to talk to anyone, just ask for me. I might be able to help you."

Douglass escaped to her own chamber, her feelings in an uproar. How could she hate a child like Lillian? Someone was manipulating her, but it could be any number of people. From what Marcus had told her, bearing the king's child meant that Lillian's future and that of her village would be assured forever. She pictured Lillian's terrified face and sighed. What difference did one frightened girl make to a future such as that?

Later that evening, Douglass was surprised when all three of her pleasure servers appeared in her chamber. Sven held up a bottle of perfumed oil.

"We decided that you needed to relax, consort."

Douglass rose up on one elbow as the men distributed the oil between themselves. Despite her miserable state, how could she not enjoy being the focus of three men's attention?

"Don't you have to be somewhere else?"

Harlan glanced at Sven. "Lady Lillian did not require our services tonight. She was dining with—"

Bron elbowed Harlan in the gut. Douglass managed a smile. "It's all right, Bron. I'm sure she and Marcus will have a delightful evening together."

"He doesn't share her bed."

Harlan's quietly spoken words made Douglass want to cry again. Marcus hadn't shared her bed since Lillian's arrival either. "I should think not. Her precious child would surely be disturbed by all that poking and prodding."

Sven grinned as he slid his oiled hands over her breasts. "Let's not worry about that, I am eager to suckle your breasts. They seem more sensitive recently."

Douglass glanced down at her chest. Not only were they more sensitive but they seemed to be getting bigger as well. All this sitting around and moping made her eat more and she was definitely getting fat. She sighed as Sven caressed her nipples, his big thumbs circling in an unhurried pattern. It was fitting that all three of her men were here tonight. She intended to leave tomorrow, despite what Marcus wanted.

Perhaps it would be easier for both of them if they were apart. Harlan kissed her mouth, his dark eyes serious, his lips gently asking for admittance. She kissed him back as Bron oiled her butt and the folds of her sex. Sven's cock brushed her cheek and she turned to take it into her mouth, loving the rough feel of him, determined to give them all pleasure before she had to leave.

Soon oil covered them all and Douglass was beyond caring whose fingers slid inside her or who touched her breasts. She'd sucked them all more than once, her mouth ached from the constant suckling but she didn't mind. They'd made her come more times than she could count, allowed her to scream and moan and cry with abandon. She settled to sleep between them, her body satiated, her mind at peace.

She was jerked out of sleep when another body joined them on the massive bed. Through half-opened eyes she saw Marcus was already naked and aroused. Her senses thrilled to life as he closed in on her, like a big cat on the hunt. He crawled up the bed, pushing his way through the other men until he crouched over her. Before she could react, he worked his stiff cock deep inside her and began to thrust. Her body, primed by hours of stimulation made no protest at his huge presence.

He pumped into her, his balls hitting her butt, his hands braced on either side of her head. She wrapped her arms around his neck and hung on as she climaxed again and again. He didn't stop, if anything his shaft seemed to grow bigger inside her. Without withdrawing he put his hands beneath her buttocks and drew her higher into his thrusts, grazing her clit with every hard stroke.

She forgot about the other men, she forgot about herself. Her whole body existed for his lovemaking, for the pounding of his hips, the gathering of his seed and the roar of completion when he finally spurted his hot come right into her very center.

He rested his head on the pillow next to hers, his breathing harsh, his heartbeat unsteady. Sven and the others had disappeared, leaving them alone. Lazily, Douglass turned to lick Marcus' neck. The scent of Lillian's perfume caught at her throat. She struggled to be free.

Marcus rolled off her and lit the lamp next to the bed before he headed for the door.

Douglass scrambled off the bed and stormed after him. She turned him back toward her. His head snapped back as she slapped him hard on the cheek.

"You smell like Lillian. Did she refuse your lovemaking so you thought you'd crawl between my thighs and work out your frustrations here?"

"You smell of four men and you seemed to be enjoying yourself quite well enough without me, consort." Marcus sneered.

She clenched her hands into fists. "I thought I was supposed to enjoy them. Isn't that why you gave them to me?" She laughed in his face. "Don't tell me you are jealous when you can fuck any woman on the planet."

Marcus drew in a sharp breath, his expression lethal.

Douglass thumped him in the chest with both of her fists. He didn't try and stop her as she pounded out her frustration against his muscled flesh. Her fists hurt and still she hit him, tears pouring down her face. She was almost glad when he caught her wrists and pressed her against his chest.

"Stop now, consort. Stop now before you hurt yourself. Hush."

"You have to let me go, Marcus. I don't want to live like this."

He stroked her hair. "I know that. It is my duty to honor the future mother of my child. But I find it impossible to be with her when I would rather be with you."

Douglass pushed away from him and sat on the side of the bed. "Then it would be better for both of us if I leave."

He came down on his knees in front of her. "You think me cruel but all my life I have been told I must have children. If I can't give my planet an heir how can I convince my people to keep on living here when the chances of having a child seem to decrease every year?" He grasped her hands. "You are a woman, you must understand the desire to hold your own child in your arms."

"I have a child, Marcus."

His whole body shuddered. "You have a child?" His expression softened. "Is that why you insist you cannot stay here with me?"

Douglass bit her lip. "Danny probably thinks I'm dead by now."

"Nay, if he truly is your son, he will be certain you will return."

"He's only five," she whispered. "He will not understand." Damn it, she wanted to weep again. What was the matter with her?

Marcus got slowly to his feet as if he had suddenly aged ten years. "Then we must get you home. If it pleases you, I will send a party of men into the Purple Desert to try and retrieve your ship's black box."

Douglass rose too, trying to ignore the pain she sensed behind Marcus' words. "You would do that for me?"

He smiled then and stroked her cheek. "If I can help reunite you with your son, I will consider myself a lucky man."

She closed the distance between them and he dragged her into his arms. Suddenly, duty and honor seemed unforgiving and harsh, their love for each other too painful to speak of.

"Thank you, my King."

Marcus stepped back and bowed. "And you, my consort."

With that, he walked away. Douglass sank back onto the sheets. She could smell Marcus' unmistakable scent on her skin and in her bed. She curled up into a ball and lay down. By granting her dearest wish, Marcus had doomed himself to a loveless future. She stuffed her fingers into her mouth to stop herself from wailing her grief aloud and rocked herself to sleep.

# Chapter Eight

∽

"Mistress Freya says I did what?"

Douglass stared at Thorlan, the chief advisor of the king's Council, as she struggled to wake up and get dressed. He was a tall man with gray hair and a long flowing beard. His eyes were the same pale watchful blue as a Siberian Husky dog.

"Mistress Freya claims you threatened the Lady Lillian."

"That's ridiculous." Douglass shoved her arm into a silk tunic and glared right back at Thorlan. Where was Sven when she needed him?

"Is it true that you visited the Lady Lillian without her mother's permission?"

Damn, the young guard must have told tales. "I didn't realize that a grown woman couldn't receive her own guests."

Thorlan inclined his head. "Our ways are different than yours. Women are expected to remain in seclusion and obey their elders." His gaze wandered over her short tunic.

Douglass tugged it down until it covered her knees. "If I offend you, perhaps you could've waited to give me this lecture until after I dressed."

He smiled. "You do not offend me at all. It is always a pleasure to see a woman's form, especially one as beautiful as yours."

"What do you want me to do?" Douglass demanded, "Apologize?"

"It's more serious than that. As mother of the future queen, Mistress Freya's word carries considerable weight."

Douglass managed a careless shrug. "I intended to take up residence in the spaceport today anyway. Does that clear up your problem?"

Thorlan frowned. "The king didn't mention this. When did he make the decision to release you from your vow?"

"I made the decision. Now if it's okay with you, I need to pack and get out of your hair. You can tell Mistress Freya I've gone. I'm sure she'll be delighted."

Two of the king's guards appeared at the entrance to her room and blocked the door. Thorlan nodded at them. "Consort, you are not taking this seriously. Mistress Freya has made a formal complaint against you. You are the king's acknowledged consort. The matter will have to be investigated by the Council."

"Fuck the Council." Douglass raised her chin. "I'm leaving." She marched up to the guards but they refused to budge. She barely controlled her desire to smash her way through, even knowing it would be useless.

Thorlan touched her shoulder. "I'll find the king. Perhaps he can make you see reason."


The first of the two suns reached its peak before Marcus managed to get to see Douglass. She sat on her bed, a scowl on her face, a packed bag at her feet. She'd braided her hair in a single plait down her back and wore more clothes than he'd ever seen on her before. Marcus ordered the guards to wait outside.

"I hear you are leaving us."

He couldn't keep the bite out of his voice. He knew they'd agreed their separation was for the best. He hadn't realized she intended to leave him the very first minute she could.

"I'm trying to, but apparently your future mother-in-law has made a formal complaint against me which has to be investigated before I can go."

Marcus dragged a chair across the carpet to sit in front of her. "Thorlan said you swore at him. I believe he was quite shocked."

She leaned forward, her hands clasped together. Purple circles under her eyes underlined her weariness and the pain in her direct gaze. "Let me go, Marcus."

He reached for her but pulled back at the last moment. "If you agree, the Council has suggested a compromise."

She continued to stare at him, the sharp intelligence in her face made him want to ignore common sense, drag her into his arms and never let go.

"What did you have to promise them?"

He smiled. "I am the king. Why should you imagine that it was I who had to compromise?"

Douglass looked unconvinced. "Whatever happens, I'm not staying here."

Marcus shifted his weight in his chair. "You can leave the palace if you agree to accompany Sven on the quest to retrieve your spacecraft."

"Why on earth would the Council let me do that?"

"Because I told them that if you managed to signal your people it would get rid of you faster." He wondered if she understood how much giving that advice had hurt him.

She bit her lip, her expression as careful as his. "That was kind of you. It will be great to get out and not to be cooped up."

To his secret relief, her lack of enthusiasm to leave appeared to match his own. "If you are out of the palace, Mistress Freya can no longer fear for her daughter's safety and Sven as my most trusted bodyguard can vouch for your behavior and prevent you from escaping."

Douglass nodded, her gaze no longer on his.

"Thorlan agreed because despite his words, he finds you fascinating."

She shrugged. "Yeah, right. It occurred to me that he was probably one of the guys who saw me naked on that first night when I became your consort."

Marcus drew a painful breath. "I release you from the vows you made that night."

She still wouldn't look at him.

He stood up and gripped the back of the ornate chair in an effort not to reach for her. "After you contact your people, Sven will wait with you at the spaceport until they come for you."

His erection brushed the back of the chair. Was she wet and ready for him as well? He cleared his throat, unable to speak as a tear glimmered on the silk of her skirts. Was this goodbye?

He inclined his head. "I wish you well, my consort."

Douglass remained on the bed, her knuckles white. "I wish you well too, my King."

Marcus walked out and found his way to his apartments. He bolted the door against Thorlan and the servants who clustered around him. His cock throbbed with unsatisfied desire. If he wanted a woman he only had to snap his fingers and one would be provided for him. The very thought made him nauseous.

He sank down into a chair and wrapped his fingers 'round his shaft. Letting Douglass go was the right thing to do. She had a child. Possibly even a man to rear that child with. The image of her with another man made him want to puke. How could he insist she stay with him when he had nothing to offer her but his love?

His cock jerked painfully within his ferocious grasp. His throat ached as if he wanted to howl and mourn like a wounded animal. He was the king, he had a planet to govern and a people to lead. Douglass challenged him like no other woman he had ever met. But her bright courage and humor would never be his to enjoy.

A knock on the door reminded him that he was needed and that a king wasn't allowed to display such grief in public. For once he yearned for the privacy to act like a simple man whose soul had just been ripped in two.

# Chapter Nine

**ဏ**

Douglass shaded her eyes and studied the vast expanse of the Purple Desert which lay before her. Sand shimmered like water as it caught light from the two suns making the landscape seem alive. Soft rounded hills that went on forever crowned the horizon. Six mounted men spread out beside her, Sven, ever vigilant, was by her side.

Their Nav-track devices seemed primitive compared to the ones she was used to on Earth. For the first time in her life Douglass truly understood the hopelessness of the old saying about needles and haystacks.

"Do we have any idea where we are heading?"

Sven unraveled his long head scarf to expose his mouth. "Yes, consort, we do. For security reasons, the crash site has been monitored ever since you arrived here." He motioned at the man in front of her.

"Karan is our best tracker. He will ensure we arrive at our destination within the next three days."

She hadn't realized they had so far to travel. Of course, her injuries from the crash had made everything seem dreamlike until she woke up to the feel of Marcus' cock against her lips...

Dammit. She had to stop thinking about him. He had chosen his royal pain in the ass path of duty and she had a fulfilling life to lead back on Earth — didn't she? At least she had Danny to love and a few close friends to help her through. Who did Marcus have? Lillian?

She wrapped her shawl around the lower half of her face and studied the terrain. Three nights in a tent in the desert with six men. She reminded herself that at least it was better than a jail cell in the palace.

Douglass shivered as the suns abruptly disappeared leaving the desert bathed in moonlight. The two white planets that orbited Valhalla were both smaller than Earth's moon but far brighter. Had she only been here for three months? It seemed longer. She had forged an unforgettable relationship with Marcus and gained the friendship of her male servers. She studied Sven's tall form as he moved around the campsite putting up the tent.

Night creatures, drawn by the lure of the lamplight, emerged from the dunes to circle the tents. Despite Sven's teasing, Douglass still hated the sound of beetles and termites scratching around in the sand beneath her sleeping bag. Danny would've been in heaven. He collected bugs like other children collected candy. Tomorrow they were due at the crash site. If they were lucky enough to find the black box, Douglass might be on her way home soon.

She sighed as Sven came to sit beside her. Nausea tugged at her senses. Never again would she experience the pleasure of being waited on hand and foot by three men. Never again would she know the extravagances of Marcus' lovemaking. She'd be back to being boring old Douglass Fraser, United Planetary Parcel Service pilot extraordinaire, trying to keep a roof over her family's head.

"Are you well, consort?"

"I'm fine, Sven." She studied his calm, rugged face in the flickering firelight. "What will happen to you and the others when I leave?"

He settled next to her on the sand and crossed his legs. "We will resume our positions in the king's bodyguard unless we are selected to serve the Lady Lillian."

"Will you mind?"

He turned to her, his gaze considering. "It has been an honor to service you, consort. If I never have the opportunity to know a woman again I will consider myself privileged to have satisfied you."

Douglass patted his arm. "I wish I could take you with me. I have loads of single girlfriends who would just love to meet a man like you."

"Your women are not all taken then?"

"No, I'd guess there are probably more women than men in the general population. It's hard to get a guy to stick around these days."

"The king told me you have a son. Does he not have a father?"

"You see, there's a case in point. Danny's father ran out on me when he found out I was pregnant."

Sven snorted. "I'm surprised your family didn't seek him out and end his existence."

Douglass suppressed a desire to laugh. "You can't go around doing things like that on Earth anymore, even if you'd like to. And anyway, it was partly my fault. If I'd listened to my family and friends I would never have gone out with him. He was a complete jerk and I refused to see it until it was too late."

"If I had a son, I would never leave him." Sven sounded stubborn, his fingers closed around the hilt of his dagger.

"As I said, you are a good man. The immature idiot who fathered Danny wasn't."

"My wife died in childbirth."

Douglass dug her fingernails into his arm. "Oh God, Sven, I'm so sorry,"

He stared into the fire. "It was many years ago. As with a lot of our women, the pregnancy did not go well with her. My son never took a breath." He let out a long sigh. "The king will make a good father."

Douglass' serene mood abruptly disintegrated. She got clumsily to her feet. "Yes, he will, won't he?" She dug her fingernails into her palms as she imagined Marcus caring for Lillian's child. Danny deserved a father like Marcus not the scumbag who had deserted him before his birth. She headed for the tent and curled up in her sleeping bag before Sven could realize she was crying.


Douglass woke to find she had wiggled free of her sleeping bag and had rolled on top of Sven's. His heavy thigh lay between her legs and she was unashamedly rubbing herself against him. One of his large hands rested lightly on her butt and held her in place. She opened her eyes to find him watching her.

"I'm sorry, Sven. It's just that..."

He smiled at her, his teeth white in the gloom of the tent they shared. "You don't need to explain, consort. I am at your service. The king gave me express orders that you were to be satisfied."

Douglass was too horny to argue with him. She'd grown far too used to having sex whenever she wanted it. She unzipped her sleeping bag and crawled into Sven's. He pulled her across his body until she straddled him. His erect cock strained the front of his leather pants. Heat radiated from his body as she leaned down and kissed him hard on the lips. He threaded his hand through her hair to hold her close as she worked on the ties of his shirt.

With a murmur of approval, he pulled off her leggings and let her sink back down against his shaft. She took off her top, freeing her breasts, and leaned forward until they brushed his face.

"Ah…consort."

He took the tip of her nipple into his mouth and sucked. She gasped at how sensitive she felt. He eased his sucking as she rocked against him, loving the feel of his leather-clad cock against her clit and pussy. She came quickly, soaking his pants with her cream.

When he suddenly sat up she only had time to grab him around the neck and hang on. He slid his hand between their bodies and cupped her mound. "Tell me what you need. Do you want my fingers or my mouth?"

She studied his intent face. "Tell me what you want, Sven." She sensed his hesitation and lightly nipped his earlobe. "Just for once, I want you to take control."

His muscles bunched under her fingers as he drew her down onto the ground and pushed her legs wide with his massive shoulders. "Then I'll finger-fuck you first and when you've come I'll use my mouth."

Douglass' sex throbbed in time to her heartbeat as he smiled down at her.

"You'll have to be quiet, consort, unless you want all the other men to come and watch. They've probably never seen a royal bodyguard fuck a real live woman."

He slid one thick finger inside her. She tried to clamp down on it.

"You need more to fill you now. The king's cock is very wide."

She glanced at the front of his pants. "So is yours."

He stroked himself through his pants. "Perhaps you'd do me the honor of sucking my cock when I allow you to stop climaxing."

Douglass licked her lips. "The honor will be all mine."

He slid another finger inside her and scissored them, widening her even further. She quivered as he curled one upward and touched her G-spot.

"You were very tight when we first took you to bed. But even then we knew you would prove an exceptional lover for the king." He added two more fingers. His thumb slowly circled her clit. "You were always so wet and welcoming. Your body was made to be caressed."

He slowly worked her, his fingers keeping a steady glide, the pressure on her clit increased with each stroke. She dug her heels into the ground, raising her hips to his as her climax grew and consumed her. The musky scent of her arousal filled the small tent as he bent to her breast. She tugged on his thick red hair.

"Kiss me, Sven."

He obliged, his mouth moving over hers with a savage intensity. Her second climax swept over her, her sheath tight around his questing fingers. Before she finished shuddering he slid downward, his tongue finding her pussy in one smooth stroke. He licked her from clit to anus, back and forth so slowly that she wanted to scream. When he buried three fingers deep in her back passage and applied his teeth to her clit she grabbed hold of his hair and held on as another ferocious climax shook through her.

With all her remaining strength, Douglass rose to her knees. She used her teeth to pull at the side lacing on Sven's soaked pants, until his cock sprang free. He groaned as she sucked him deep into her mouth. She cradled his balls in her hand and used the tip of her finger to press on the sweet spot behind the head. He groaned, fisting his hands in her long hair.

"Harder, consort, suck me harder."

She'd always known his sexual tastes ran to the rougher side. Without the constraints of the other men around him she was shocked to realize she wanted to give him more. She used her teeth on his delicate foreskin. Let him watch the play of her lips and tongue, enjoyed the shudders that ran through his body. When he thrust urgently back into her mouth she penetrated the tight bud of his anus and headed for his prostate.

He growled, his hand in her hair growing tighter and more demanding as she pleasured him. He came with a mighty roar, his come spilling down her throat as she continued to suck him. Douglass' pussy clenched along with him, missing the thrust of a cock, missing Marcus' massive presence.

Sven put his hands around her waist and drew her into his arms, his chest was still heaving as if he'd run a race. "Thank you, consort." His semi-erect cock slid against her belly as he held her tight. Douglass wanted to give him more. She pushed at his chest and he immediately released her.

Slowly she turned around and went down on all fours, her butt touching his thighs. She arched her back and pressed the swell of her buttocks into his rapidly hardening shaft. His recovery rate had always been impressive. "The king said I have the right to have you inside me."

Silence greeted her provocative words. She turned her head to look at him. One hand gripped his swollen cock, his expression was unreadable.

"I will not defile your womb, consort. That is for the pleasure of the king and his seed."

Douglass ran a finger between her butt cheeks, stopping at the bud of her anus. "Here, Sven. Would you like to fuck me here?"

His hands clamped on her hips, his cock rubbed the small of her back. When he finally spoke he sounded hoarse. "I am a big man. I do not wish to cause you pain."

Douglass thought about the slight roughness of his handling, how it would feel to have him buried deep inside her. Cream gushed out of her pussy. She slid her hand between her legs and pushed the thick cream back toward her anus. She heard him swallow hard, the wet crown of his shaft nudged lower.

"Please, Sven." She circled her anus, dipped her creamed finger inside it.

With a groan, his cock pushed her fingers out of the way. She let out her breath as he penetrated her inch by slow inch. He was almost as big as Marcus. She waited as his fingers brushed her buttocks.

His fingers closed on her nipple as he slid farther in. They tightened when his cock could go no farther. With a gentleness that surprised her, he kissed her neck. "You do me great honor, consort. I never thought to feel like this again."

Douglass concentrated on the rough tug of his fingers on her nipple, the subtle rocking of his hips as he moved within her. She closed her eyes and imagined that Marcus lay under her, his cock wedged firmly in her aching sex, his strokes the reverse of Sven's. With a frustrated moan she grabbed Sven's hand and flattened it against her mound.

"Touch me, here, make me come for you."

He stuffed all four of his fingers inside her and increased the pace of his thrusts until she felt herself climax. His desperate breathing sounded loud in her ears as he came with a yell that must have awakened every living thing in the desert around them. He slumped against her, pushing her to the floor with his greater weight.

With a sigh he rolled off her and remained on his back staring up at the roof of the tent. "Thank you, consort. I will remember this night for the rest of my life."

Douglass arranged herself against his side and pulled the remaining sleeping bag over them both. Okay, Sven could never be Marcus but he was certainly better than anything she'd be getting back on Earth.

# Chapter Ten

** හ**

"Consort, you are not making sense."

Sven frowned at Douglass as she laced up her boots and braided her hair into a thick plait down her back.

"I have to come to the site with you. I'm the only person who really understands what everything means."

"The king did not mean you to expose yourself to the rough villagers here. They don't see many women during their lifetimes, especially not out of seclusion. It's possible that they might try and overwhelm us and carry you off with them."

Douglass stood up and put on her jacket. "I'm sure you can protect me, Sven." She marched out of the tent before he could say another word. He caught up with her before she mounted her *wulfrun*.

"If there is trouble, there is a way I can use to convince the men not to fear you."

She shrugged out of his grip and mounted. "Then do it."

His rare smile transformed his face. "You might not like it."

Douglass stared at him suspiciously. "If it comes to a choice between finding the black box and surviving, I'll put up with whatever it is."

Sven bowed. "Thank you, consort."

Douglass and her party reached the site to find half a dozen men dressed in the colorful uniform of the local town guard awaiting them. Sven helped her dismount.

"Cover your head, consort. These men are from Lady Lillian's home village. They might be hostile to you."

"Why?"

Sven looked exasperated. "Because tales of your beauty and the king's love for you have been circulating ever since the crash. The men might view you as a threat to the king's future wife."

Douglass forced her face into an unassuming smile and pulled her scarf over her hair. "Great. Perhaps it might help if you let them know that finding the black box transmitter will see me on my way, permanently."

After a noncommittal grunt, Sven went over to talk to the leader of the Hammersford men. Douglass took her first good look at the crash site. Her ship lay in several pieces, scattered over the undulating purple sand. The rear section was gone, disintegrated by the intense heat when the engines had caught fire.

She shivered as she walked slowly forward. Her memories of the crash resurfaced in sudden clarity. Landing in the sand had probably saved her life. The center of the craft, where the pilot's seat was located, seemed relatively unscathed. She moved closer and bounced off a solid wall of muscle.

"Woman, get back."

Douglass took her time assessing the man who blocked her path. Despite his size, he was young, his beard more fluffy than thick.

"It's my spacecraft. I have a perfect right to look at it."

He spat in the sand. "You should not speak directly to me. You should be ashamed of yourself."

Douglass let her head scarf fall to her shoulders. "I am perfectly capable of deciding whom I can talk to, thanks. Just because your planet has some ridiculous antiquated notions doesn't mean you have a right to stop me doing anything I want."

He refused to budge. Without taking her eyes off him, Douglass yelled, "Sven!"

He appeared behind her in an instant. "Yes, king's consort?"

"Will you tell this jerk to get out of my way?"

Sven came closer and pulled her against his chest. One of his hands cupped her breast. "Of course, consort. Your wishes are paramount." He fixed the younger man with a piercing glare. "You do not wish to upset the king's chosen consort, do you?"

The man stepped back. His gaze riveted on Sven's hand as he stroked and fondled her breast.

"If you accompany her, I suppose she can proceed."

Sven kissed Douglass' throat and closed his finger and thumb around her hardened nipple, displaying it to the sentry. "Of course."

He guided Douglass past the sentry toward the spacecraft, one arm around her shoulders.

"What the hell was that all about?" Douglass hissed.

"I told you I might have to get around them."

Her nipple still throbbed from his sudden attention. "So you felt me up to distract him?"

Sven stopped walking and frowned. "Felt you up? I have no idea what you mean, consort. I just made sure he knew that I provided for you. He needed to believe you were guarded and guided by a male and not acting independently."

Douglass gritted her teeth. "If I was staying on this planet I'd be talking to your king about changing a few things around here." She stomped away from Sven and stared at the remnants of her pilot's chair. The black leather seat cover hung in shreds displaying the foam innards. A triangular metal cage and the spray on foam had protected her during the unscheduled descent. It remained in place around her seat and console. Thank goodness she had already delivered all her cargo.

"What does this black box look like?" Sven stood on the opposite side of the ship, scanning the desert.

"It's usually about forty centimeters long and twenty wide." During her pilot training the instructors had emphasized that the black box would always be located in the most secure part of the craft. Douglass got down on her knees and crawled carefully into the wreckage.

"Consort! It isn't safe."

Sven's urgent shout came to late to stop her. The acrid scent of burned metal and sand rose in choking clouds as she slid her hand under the captain's seat. Her fingers closed around something substantial. With all her strength she grabbed it and tried to pull it free.

"Dammit." She looked up to find Sven sprawled alongside her. "It's stuck. Can you get it out?"

She retreated to allow him access to the small space. After two attempts, Sven emerged with the bright red box in his hands. He patted his clothes to remove the thick dusting of charred materials and sand.

"This cannot be what you seek. It's not black."

Douglass took the box from him and laid it carefully on the ground. A single white light blinked on one side of it. "The black box doesn't always have to be black. It's just a catch-all name."

Sven snorted. "It also explains why nobody thought it important to remove this from under the seat and save us a journey."

Douglass ignored him as he crouched down next to her in the sand. The box had an old-fashioned locking system which was programmed to respond to her personal identity code. She glanced up as a shadow blocked the sun. The leader of the Hammersford guards stood over her.

"Lord Sven. Perhaps you might bring the king's consort into our tents. She might feel more comfortable there rather than out here where all can see her."

Sven caught Douglass' eye. "May I escort you inside?"

She stood up and handed the box to him. "Thank you, Sven."

To Douglass' dismay, four of the Hammersford men insisted on entering the small tent with her. She waited until Sven placed the box on the table before she approached it. A murmur went around the table.

Sven stayed close to her, one arm sliding around her waist as she pressed in her code. The box opened to display two green lights. Douglass let out a breath.

"This might explain why nobody's come to rescue me yet. The UPPS probably couldn't locate me when the primary alarms on the ship went off because they have no data on this planet. And it looks as if this secondary signal in the black box didn't go off at all. The landing was probably too soft. It's possible that they needed the second set of signals to identify exactly where I ended up."

Sven looked over her shoulder, his fingers toyed with the fastenings on her tunic top. "What do the lights mean, consort?"

One of the older Hammersford men laughed in a kindly fashion. "How would she know? She is hardly designed to understand science. Women should concentrate on breeding and being pleased by their men."

Douglass tried to ignore him and concentrate on Sven. "The green light on the left means that the memory matrix, which is a record of the journey, is still intact. The green light on the right is for the accelerometer."

Sven's hand slipped inside her tunic and pulled it down exposing half of her breast to the room. The muttering stopped. "I do not understand this word, accelerometer; can you explain?" His fingers teased at her nipple.

"It measures speed. It can tell whether the spacecraft speeds up or slows down." Douglass swallowed hard as his fingers worked over her exposed flesh, cupping her breast, using the pad of his thumb to arouse her nipple, letting them all see her helpless response.

"If the craft is in an accident, this evidence of a sudden dramatic increase or decrease in speed activates an emergency signal which will be sent back to my home planet."

Sven continued to stroke her breast, baring it completely now. His erect cock pressed against the small of her back. He rocked his hips in time to his stroking. "But you believe the signal wasn't sent."

"It doesn't look like it." God, it was hard to breathe when Sven touched her like this. Exactly when had she decided it was a turn-on to enjoy other men watching her being caressed so intimately? "As I said, it's possible the landing on the sand was too soft."

Sven drew the cloth away from her other breast. He tugged on her nipples until they were equally stiff. "How do you suggest we get the signal to work?" He bent his head and brought her breast to his mouth, sucking hard.

"I...don't know."

He looked up from his task, releasing her nipple with a soft pop. "Do any of you have a suggestion?"

The oldest man stepped forward. His gaze fixed on Douglass' breasts. "Perhaps if we threw the box to the ground, it might activate the signal."

"That is a good suggestion." Sven gestured to the man to come closer. "I will do this task if you continue to pleasure the king's consort." He placed the man's hand on Douglass' breast.

Douglass barely noticed the man's respectful touch as she waited to see what would happen. Sven dropped the box from above his head. Neither light changed. He picked it back up and set it on the table. With a bow to the older man, he resumed his place beside Douglass.

"Does anyone else have an idea?"

As if he couldn't help himself. Sven slid his hand down between Douglass' thighs and cupped her mound. He murmured his approval at her slick wetness.

"Something more violent, perhaps. Something more like a real crash." The young bearded guard who had blocked Douglass' way spoke up.

Sven nodded his approval. "Another excellent suggestion." He removed his hands from Douglass. "But for this we need to be outside." Before she could follow him out, he led her over to the young guard. "Stay by the king's consort, please. Touch her if she asks you to."

Douglass remained in the doorway to the tent while Sven stripped off his tunic and unsheathed his massive sword. He tossed the black box to one of his men. "On the count of three, throw this at me."

The box flew through the air and met the flat blade of Sven's mighty sword. He buffeted it with such force that it sailed toward one of the low rock formations and hit it with a resounding crash. With a roar of triumph, Sven strode across to the box and picked it up. The light on the right side now blinked red.

Douglass grinned at Sven. "I think that did the trick." Her smile faded as he came toward her. "Now all we have to do is get back to the spaceport and wait."

# Chapter Eleven

## ༣

Douglass paced the small control room at the spaceport, her gaze glued to the horizon. She'd been at the station for almost three days. Five days since the emergency beacon was activated. Sven sat on the console behind her, arms crossed over his chest.

"Consort, the operator said the signal he received was very faint. It could take several more days for another craft to reach here."

She smiled at his less than patient tone. It was Sven's job to see that she remained in custody until she left the planet. Was he eager to get rid of her and return to the king? He shifted position and frowned at her. "Consort..."

"You can go if you like, Sven. I'm sure the port operator would be quite happy to watch over me."

Sven shot to his feet. He reached her in two angry strides and took her by the shoulders. He gave her a firm shake. "I will wait with you. I promised the king I would see you safely restored to your people."

It was an old argument; one Douglass knew she had no chance of winning. Thick nausea crawled up the back of her throat as she scanned the empty blue sky. What if no one came? After three months they might have given up on her.

A warning code crackled over the archaic com system followed by a female voice. "Planet Valhalla, this is the United Planetary Parcel Service ship *Eagle One*. Please copy."

After a startled glance at Douglass the operator punched some buttons. "This is Planet Valhalla, over."

"Request permission to land, Planet Valhalla. We believe you have a misplaced package of ours."

With a shriek of joy, Douglass threw herself into Sven's arms and let him swing her around in a circle. "It worked! They got it!"

By the time the huge spacecraft set down, everyone in the starport and the immediate vicinity had gathered to watch. Douglass waited anxiously at the bottom of the ship glideway. The first figure to emerge wore a brown jumpsuit with four stars glittering on her chest. She shaded her eyes against the brightness.

"Douglass, is that you?" With a whoop, the woman ran down the slope and hugged Douglass hard.

"Marge! How did you get this assignment?" Douglass hugged her old friend from pilot training school, tears already streamed down her face.

"Did you think I'd let anyone else come?" Marge demanded, her gaze fierce, her blue eyes suspiciously bright. Marge was Danny's godmother and Douglass' strongest supporter. "I've been keeping an eye on Danny for you. He'll be so excited to have you back!"

Douglass grabbed Marge's hands. "He's okay? He's really okay?"

"Well, he's been missing you like crazy and I've probably spoiled him so much that you'll ground him for the rest of his life, but, yeah, he's okay. You can talk to him later on the link and find out for yourself."

"Consort, is this female bothering you?"

Douglass turned as Sven came up behind her. She smiled at him. "Not at all, she's come to rescue me."

Marge gazed at Sven's bare chest and ferocious expression. Her gaze dropped to his tight leather pants which were the only thing he wore apart from his boots. "Wow. Does he belong to you? He seems a mite possessive."

"He's kind of like my bodyguard." Douglass winked at Sven as they swept past him. "He's quite sweet when you get to know him, really."

"I bet he is. In my experience, the sourer they look the sweeter they taste."

Marge grinned at Douglass. "Perhaps I didn't need to rescue you after all."


Inside the best suite the small hotel could provide, Marge relaxed enough to remove her jacket as Douglass gave her an edited version of what had happened since the crash.

Marge sighed. "We'll have to pick up the pieces of your craft. UPSS will want to analyze the data."

"I can give you the coordinates." Douglass took note of Sven's glare. "It might be better if you send an all-male team to the site. The locals aren't used to seeing women out and about in the open."

Marge sipped at her *ozan* juice. "Yeah, I noticed that when I reviewed the data on this godforsaken planet. Men outnumber women by about fifty to one." She grinned at Douglass. "Nice odds if you can get it."

Sven got up and stalked into the bedroom. Douglass winced as he slammed the door.

"God, he's gorgeous when he's angry," Marge breathed. "Is he mad because you are leaving?"

"I don't think so. It's probably because you referred to this planet as godforsaken. They take their gods very seriously here."

Marge leaned forward and touched Douglass' knee. "But you are okay, aren't you? You look really well. In fact, you look better than ever."

"I've been treated like a princess." More like a queen Douglass wanted to say but she didn't want to complicate matters too much. Her planet might take a serious view of her being required to have sex with several men. She thought of Marcus. Would news of the ship's arrival have reached him yet? Would he bother to come and say goodbye?

Marge got to her feet. "The med lab wants to run a few tests on you to make sure you haven't picked up anything unpleasant from your stay here. Can you come aboard now?"

Douglass glanced at the closed bedroom door. In his present mood would Sven care if she went without him? She headed for the exit after Marge as quickly as she could.


The large medical lab on the ship was empty apart from her and the female doctor. Douglass stripped off her clothes and put on the scratchy green cover-nothing gown laid out on the bed. She hated the smell of disinfectant and the glaring whiteness of the walls. It reminded her all too forcibly that her erotic interlude was over and that it was time to return the realities of her less than romantic life.

"Hi, Douglass, I'm Doctor Barbara Jensen."

Douglass shook the doctor's cold hand and watched warily as she laid out a variety of instruments on a tray. Her hair was pure white, her skin a pale coffee color; she could've been any age from thirty to fifty. A slight prick on Douglass' wrist indicated the blood test was complete. She studied the small puncture hole as it seamlessly healed itself.

"I'll just get this analyzed."

Douglass sighed and stared at the ceiling. After a few long moments she allowed her attention to drift to the doctor who stood in front of a diagnostic screen.

Doctor Jensen's back stiffened and her shoulders crept up toward her ears as diagnostic figures spiked with red flashes spilled onto the screen. Even with her small knowledge of medicine, Douglass had seen enough medical dramas on the entertainment tube to tell her something was wrong. When the doctor returned, she sat beside Douglass and took her hand.

"There are two things you need to know about the test results."

Douglass struggled to sit up. "Good or bad?"

"It depends." Doctor Jensen hesitated, her brown eyes fixed on Douglass. "The first thing is that this planet's atmosphere contains very high levels of a toxic chemical called chlordane."

"Is it dangerous?"

"It can be. Prolonged exposure can cause cancer, brain damage and fertility problems."

Keen to be distracted from her own predicament Douglass said, "I wonder if that's why the people here can't seem to have children?"

"Possibly. It's something we can look into. But to get back to you. There are drugs we could give you to combat the effects of chlordane, but…"

Douglass studied the doctor's kind face. "But…?"

"That brings me to the second thing." She sighed. "Did you know you are eight weeks pregnant?"

Douglass simply stared at her as a million small intuitive memories finally collided in her head to form a cohesive mass. She'd assumed her sore breasts and queasiness were a result of her new diet and overactive sex life. Her first pregnancy had been nothing like this. She jumped off the gurney.

"Excuse me!"

She only just made it to the bathroom before she retched. When she finally stopped, Doctor Jensen crouched beside her, a wet cloth in her hand. After several deep breaths, Douglass allowed herself to be led back into the main lab.

A commotion outside the lab made them both stop and stare. Sven kicked his way through the door, two security guards hanging off his arms. He spied Douglass.

"Consort, are you well? Did these space travelers hurt you?"

Doctor Jensen whistled an appreciative tune. "Is this the potential father? He looks like a nice healthy specimen."

Sven growled at the doctor as he flexed his biceps and bounced one of the security guards against the wall. Within a minute, as sirens wailed and lights flashed, Marge arrived with a second security team. She pointed her weapon at Sven.

"Douglass, if you can't get him to behave, I'll have to knock him out."

Douglass took hold of Sven's arm and detached him from the guards.

"It's okay, Sven, I'm fine." She pushed at his chest until he sat down with a thump on the gurney, hands fisted at his sides. "Marge, can you get everybody out of here? I need to talk to you and the doctor."

Marge snapped into efficiency mode and had the room cleared in ten seconds. Douglass' ears continued to ring long after the alarms were silenced. Marge shut the door with a bang and frowned at Sven who remained seated on the gurney.

"You're scarcely decent, Douglass." She cast an eye over Douglass' crumpled paper gown. "Do you want muscle man in here?"

"I will not leave the king's consort," Sven growled. "I am responsible for her safety."

Douglass patted his leather-clad knee. "Of course you can stay. It's not as if he hasn't seen me naked before."

Sven brought her hand to his lips. "Naked and ready for sex, consort, as is my right and my pleasure."

Douglass smiled briefly at him and then turned back to Marge and Doctor Jensen who wore identical expressions of intense interest. She shrugged. "It's not quite how it sounds. Let me explain."

By the time she finished telling them a fairly cleaned-up version of her interesting lifestyle and sexual habits on Planet Valhalla, Marge was staring at her in admiration.

"Hell, Douglass, I never thought you had it in you."

"Neither did I. But I can highly recommend it." Douglass smiled—apart from the bit when you fall in love with a king who has to put duty ahead of you.

Doctor Jensen looked thoughtful. "So in theory, any one of the four men you had consensual sex with could be the father of your child."

Douglass bit her lip. Perhaps she should've been more specific. "It depends on what you mean by sex. Only one of the men actually…"

"What the king's consort is trying to say is that only the king was privileged to plant his seed in her womb." Sven gave Douglass a helpful wink.

Doctor Jensen didn't seem pleased. "In theory, that's true but semen has a mind of its own sometimes." She got up. "We'll have to take DNA samples from all of the men and from the fetus." She smiled reassuringly at Sven. "We can start with you."

Douglass laid a protective hand over her belly. "Are you sure that won't hurt the baby?"

"I wouldn't suggest it if it wasn't safe. We also need to check the fetus for any abnormalities due to this toxic climate."

A wave of dizziness swept over Douglass. Half an hour ago she hadn't even known she was pregnant, now she felt as protective as a lioness with her cub. An image of Lillian's swollen stomach and puffy face came over her.

"Doctor Jensen, we'll have to ask the king's permission to visit the palace and persuade him to allow DNA samples to be taken." She frowned. "As far as I know, the technology doesn't exist on this planet. So he and the Council might take some convincing."

She glanced at Sven. "Perhaps you could take a message to the king and ask if we might arrange a meeting with him." She didn't want to turn up uninvited and risk Mistress Freya insisting she was thrown into prison. It was also possible that Marcus might simply refuse to see her.

Sven got up and bowed. "It would ban an honor, consort."

Douglass grabbed his arm. "Don't say anything about the possibility of a baby yet, please?" She searched his face, sensed his reluctance. "For all we know this could just be a false alarm. I would much rather we had our facts straight before we faced the king."

Sven nodded. "I promise, consort. But only because I do not want the king to be disappointed." She kissed his cheek as he patted her butt, his fingers stealing under the crumpled gown to caress her flesh. "I will return as soon as I can."

After he turned to leave, Douglass found Doctor Jensen's fascinated gaze was fixed on Sven's departing back. She cleared her throat and the doctor jumped.

"Before you begin the tests, can I ask you about another woman here who is pregnant?"

"Of course, Douglass, but remember I'm unable to treat any of the people on this planet without express permission from the king and his Council. Do you think the king would allow it?"

Douglass allowed herself a small smile. "Definitely. After all, the results could determine the future of his planet."

# Chapter Twelve

## ഇ

Marcus frowned as he strode into the small audience chamber. Douglass' request to see him and the Council before her departure had surprised him. He'd half hoped she would simply leave. The thought of seeing her again was far too painful to contemplate.

Earlier, Thorlan had tried to remind him that Douglass was still under suspicion of harming Lillian and needed his blessing to leave the planet. Marcus snarled at him to go away. Four security guards, dressed in the same brown garb Douglass had worn on her arrival, waited by the wide-open doors. In the center of the room stood three women.

He recognized Douglass immediately even though she'd changed into a brown garment and tied back her hair. Sven stood behind her, his arms crossed over his chest. Marcus took up his position in the center of the dais and sat on his throne.

The older of the two remaining females stepped forward. "Greetings, King Marcus Blood Axe of Planet Valhalla. I am Doctor Barbara Jensen, chief physician on board the UPPS ship *Eagle One*."

Marcus inclined his head. "You are most welcome, doctor."

He turned his attention to the other woman who wore another of the unflattering brown outfits, although hers was covered with gold braid and stars.

"Greetings, Sire. I am Marge Jones, Captain of the *Eagle One*."

"Captain, it is a pleasure. What can I do for you?"

By Odin, all three women looked very serious. Had they come to seek reparation for Douglass' long stay on Valhalla? Did they think he had harmed her in any way?

The doctor cleared her throat. "Perhaps we might speak with you in private first, Sire. The matter is a delicate one."

Marcus frowned. "If that is your wish, I will dismiss all of the Council except Thorlan." He waited until everyone, including the security guards from the ship filed out. Douglass' face was flushed and she seemed to be avoiding his gaze. Was she in trouble because of her behavior on Valhalla? She'd told him the sexual mores on Earth were more restrictive than here.

He realized the doctor waited for his attention. "Please, doctor, tell me your concerns."

"I understand from talking to Douglass, that your medical facilities do not have access to DNA testing."

"That is true. We are a small agricultural world. We don't have the money to spend on such things." He tried not to sound defensive. "Douglass mentioned this DNA to me. What does it do?"

Doctor Jensen smiled, revealing the serene beauty of her face. "It is the essence of life. It tells a scientist the genetic makeup of a human being. It can reveal the identity of a child's parents."

Marcus felt as if a *wulfrun* had kicked him in the gut. He jumped down from the platform and headed for Douglass. He tried to keep his voice down as he confronted her. "Did you bring your doctor here to prove whether Lillian carries my child? Did you wish to destroy whatever little hope for happiness I have left before you desert me?"

Douglass put her hands on her hips. "That's hardly fair. Lillian is sick. She needs medical attention. Last time I saw her she was too scared to tell the physicians how badly she felt because she was too afraid of you."

Marcus glared down at her. "That is ridiculous."

"Why don't you let Doctor Jensen examine Lillian while she is here and set your mind at rest?" Douglass raised her chin. "And if you really want to stop being a coward and find out if the child she carries is yours, you can do that too."

For a heartbeat, Marcus fought the urge to shake his consort until her teeth rattled. "I am no coward." He bowed at the doctor. "If you wish to examine Lillian, go ahead."

The doctor touched his arm. "If it isn't too much trouble, Sire. I would appreciate a sample of your blood. It will help me with my diagnosis."

Marcus continued to glower at Douglass over the doctor's head as she pricked his thumb to draw the blood.

"Thank you, Sire. Now can you show me the way to the Lady Lillian's apartments?"


Lillian's bedchamber was shrouded in darkness and smelled of stale perfume and spoiled fruit. After the drapes were drawn back, Marcus couldn't deny that Lillian was ill. He remembered his first sight of her, gleaming with health, the slightness of her limbs, the shine of her hair. Now her face and body seemed swollen, her hair lank and lifeless.

Why hadn't anyone told him? He glanced at Lillian's mother and his physicians who were clustered in the corner of the room. Perhaps Douglass was right. Perhaps they hadn't wanted to worry him, more concerned that the baby survived than in protecting the mother.

Doctor Jensen talked quietly with Lillian and then turned to Marcus. "It would help, Sire, if we could be left alone while I complete my tests."

Deep in thought, Marcus walked out into the brightly lit sitting area. Mistress Freya was sobbing, whether in fear for her daughter or fear for her loss of status, he wasn't inclined to ask. Douglass came and sat beside him.

"Marcus, please don't think I did this for myself. I was worried about Lillian when I last saw her. I asked Doctor Jensen for her advice and she thought it best she paid Lillian a visit."

"I appreciate your concern for my wife-elect." He glanced at her quickly. "I didn't realize she was ill. Recently, I've only been allowed to visit her for relatively short periods of time."

Douglass sighed. "I'm not blaming you, Marcus."

He laughed, the sound grim in his own ears. "That's all right because I already blame myself."

She touched his wrist. "Doctor Jensen wants to talk to you about the planet's environment. She might be able to help you and your people."

The distance in her voice and the touch of her fingers made his blood heat. He struggled not to grab hold of her and kiss her until she melted into his arms. How could she sit so close to him and talk about matters that made no mention of the state of her feelings? It was if she'd already filed him away in her memories and was ready to move on.

"That is interesting. I will look forward to her setting my backward planet to rights." He couldn't keep the bitterness out of his voice. "It was a good day for us when you crashed, wasn't it?"

Her fingers slid off his wrist as if he had bitten them. "Just listen to her, Marcus, that's all I ask."

150

She walked away from him, her head held high and rejoined her crewmates. Marcus got to his feet just as Doctor Jensen reappeared and beckoned him closer.

"Lillian has a condition called pre-eclampsia."

Marcus raised an eyebrow. "What is that?"

Doctor Jensen sipped her juice. "It's a condition that occurs during pregnancy when blood pressure is raised too high."

Ah, he knew about blood pressure. "What effect does it have on the mother and child?"

"If it's allowed to go untreated, the mother can experience visual disturbances, mental dullness and in the late stages, even fits. It's also a cause of premature birth."

"Can you treat her?"

"Yes, I can. I'll show your physicians the techniques they need and ensure they have the ability to prescribe the necessary drugs." She squeezed Marcus' hand. "She will be fine. The baby should be born safely in about twelve weeks."

Marcus frowned. "That is still too early. By my calculations she is only about thirteen weeks along."

Doctor Jensen released his hand. "I'm sorry, Sire, but the scan dates confirm she is already twenty-four weeks pregnant. Pre-eclampsia doesn't usually manifest itself until week twenty."

"Then the babe cannot be mine." A mingled sense of relief and despair washed over him. He tried to keep his response light. "It explains why she practically raped me."

"Your DNA doesn't match the child's either, Sire."

He studied her sympathetic face. "So Douglass was right after all."

"Perhaps you should say that to Douglass rather than me."

Marcus kissed her hand. "I'd rather talk to you. She told me you have some ideas about what is wrong with this planet."

Doctor Jensen got up. "If you wish, I'll present my findings to you and the Council tomorrow before we take our leave. I need to attend to my patient now."

He grimaced. "If you permit, I'll come with you. I believe it's time to discover who the real father of Lillian's baby might be."


Lillian sat alone on the massive bed, her knees drawn up to her chin, her arms encircling them. At least the drapes had been opened and fresh air scented with blossoms circulated in the room. When Lillian saw Marcus, she hid her face like a child. He sat gingerly beside her on the bed without touching her.

"Have you come to send me down to the dungeons?"

Marcus fought a smile at her tragic tone. "I don't have any dungeons here. And why would I treat a woman who carries a child like that?"

She lifted her head, her eyes were red and swollen with tears. "Because I lied to you. Because you are the king."

He sought for words to calm her obvious anxiety. "I can understand why you lied. It was a great thing for your village when your mother realized you were with child. As far as she was concerned, the child had to be mine, didn't it?"

Lillian nodded. "I never meant for it to go this far. So many times I wanted to speak up and tell them the truth but I was too afraid." She fixed her gaze on him. "You will not punish my village for my sins, will you?"

"Nay, there will be no punishments handed out to anyone." He tried to give her a reassuring smile. "A genuine mistake was made and no harm was done."

She had no notion that her actions might spell the end of hope for his people. He was almost too weary to go on pretending that all would be well. His planet would die now. He wouldn't be exercising his right to bed the newest crop of virgins ever again. He thought of the heir he would never have. Bitterly regretted the shame he had brought on his family and his ancestors.

Lillian started to cry. "You are too kind to me, Sire. I knew I was pregnant the night they brought me to you. I made sure you had no choice but to mate with me."

He studied her then, felt the strength of her will beneath her feminine softness. Since Douglass' arrival his preconceived ideas about the fragility of women had changed forever.

"The man who fathered the child, did he not wish to marry you?"

Lillian knelt up, her expression indignant. "Of course he did, but the Elders had already decided that I was to be their tribute to you. I feared to shame my family by admitting I was no longer a virgin."

Marcus rubbed the bridge of his nose as a headache descended. "Perhaps you might have shared this information with me before we engaged in this farce."

She stared at him as if he were speaking a language she couldn't understand. "You are the king. I believed you would kill me if I didn't service you."

He resisted an urge to smash something. Douglass was right, this was no way for a woman to feel, forced to use her sexuality to please her family and her king.

"The man who fathered your child. Does he have a name?"

Lillian bit her lip. "You will not hurt him?"

Marcus held tight to the last strands of his patience. Whatever he did, he would always be an ogre in Lillian's eyes. "I will not hurt him, I give you my word."

"His name is Randall. We grew up together. His father is one of my father's bodyguards."

There was no need for Marcus to ask if she loved the man, her dreamy expression gave that away in an instant.

"And he still lives in Hammersford?"

"Aye, he still lives there, although he managed to secure a position as one of my bodyguards. He is here in the palace now, Sire."

Marcus mentally reviewed the men who had accompanied Lillian from Hammersford. One man in particular stood out. He had never seen him smile.

"Is Randall black-haired and tall? Does he carry his sword on his left?"

"That is him." Lillian's mouth trembled. "I know we should not have fallen in love. We tried to do our duty by our families but it was too hard." She lifted her gaze to Marcus. "I was taught not to look for love and to value my fertility and use it to better my family above anything else. I never expected to love one man so much that I was prepared to lie even to my king."

Her words struck an answering chord deep in Marcus' gut. How could he fault her when he had contemplated giving up everything if he could just keep Douglass by his side?

He wiped a tear from her cheek. "Love is a gift, Lillian, don't turn away from it." He glanced at Doctor Jensen. "If

154

Lillian is well enough, perhaps you would allow her to be reunited with the father of her child."

He patted Lillian's hand and left her suite. She made him feel old and jaded. In the anteroom he spied Randall still scowling at him. He walked across to him, watching in grim amusement as Randall's face turned ashen and he fell to his knees.

"Yes, my King?"

Marcus studied the top of his head. "Randall of Hammersford, I wish to bestow a gift on you." He paused as the room went quiet. "The Lady Lillian needs a father for her child and who better suited for that task than the man who planted the seed in the first place. I intend to bestow a dowry on the lady to celebrate her fertility. Your marriage will be solemnized tomorrow in front of my chief counselors."

Randall bent forward and kissed his feet. "Thank you, Sire." He raised his head, his brown eyes pleading. "She meant no harm. She isn't very strong."

Marcus stepped back, aware of Douglass staring at him from the corner of the room. "She is stronger than you think, Randall. Take my advice, never underestimate a woman."

# Chapter Thirteen

ஒ

After an uncomfortable night's sleep in the palace guest quarters, Douglass found Harlan and Bron and persuaded them to visit Doctor Jensen. While she waited for them to return, she thought about Marcus and how he had reunited the two young lovers. From gossip overheard around the palace, she knew that people had wondered if the king would follow the ancient laws and put the young couple to death. How typical of Marcus to understand their predicament and treat them with compassion.

She continued to pace the apartment until Doctor Jensen came to find her. To her relief, the good doctor was smiling.

"After meeting all these prime healthy males I understand why you were so happy here." She chuckled as she sat down on the couch next to Douglass. "They even offered, with your permission, of course, to relieve my sexual tensions. It's been a long time since anyone half decent-looking has offered to do that."

Douglass tried to smile as nausea clutched at her throat. Doctor Jensen sighed.

"I'm sorry, dear, here I am drooling over a bunch of young studs and you need to know which one of them is the father of your child." Doctor Jensen took her hand. "The king's DNA matches that of your child."

Douglass almost fell off the couch with relief. "That's great, isn't it?" She bit her lip. "And do you think the pregnancy stands a chance of being successful?"

"So far, it's looking good, but even if the king agrees to clean up the planet's atmosphere, I wouldn't recommend you stay here for the duration."

"I thought you might say that." Douglass smoothed a hand over her belly. "But I have to tell him."

Doctor Jensen laughed. "You are a very brave woman. Although beneath that rather ferocious exterior I believe the king to have a remarkably fine mind. Perhaps you might wait and break the happy news after I've told him about the toxic chemical dump this planet has become. He might need something to cheer him up."

Douglass got up and hugged the doctor tight. "I'm sorry for all the extra work. Thanks for doing this."

Doctor Jensen nudged her as they walked toward the Council chamber. "Are you kidding? I wouldn't have missed this for the world. It's the most exciting time I've had in years. I should be thanking you."

As they advanced into the chamber, Douglass found a seat next to Marge. She fixed her gaze on Marcus and Thorlan who stood at the top of the room waiting for Doctor Jensen.

Marcus listened to the doctor in growing disbelief. How in Thor's name had his planet become a health hazard? After she finished her speech, he stood up.

"Doctor Jensen, I haven't imported any chlordane onto the planet during my reign. Are you sure this is the cause of all our ills?"

"Unfortunately, Sire, chlordane's effects are very long-lasting. One of your predecessors could have used the pesticide many years ago. The effects linger in the soil, penetrate the fabric of buildings and eventually make their way into the air."

Thorlan cleared his throat. "I believe your grandfather, Thorkill the Strong, ordered something like this." He bowed at Doctor Jensen. "In those days, our countryside was overrun by termites and beetles, which destroyed most of our crops. Thorkill knew that in order to survive our planet needed to become an agricultural provider for the new wave of space exploration and settlement."

Marcus nodded at Thorlan. "Perhaps you might verify this information, although it sounds as if you might be right. Our problems have definitely grown worse over the past fifty years." He felt sick. Of course, his people had borne the brunt of it, working in the fields, while he remained in relative health and safety behind the palace walls. He took a quick survey of the room, deliberately ignoring the crew from the *Eagle One*. Most of his Council looked shocked but resigned to the fact that their king was taking advice from an elderly female.

He turned back to Doctor Jensen who sat quietly in her seat. "What can we do to stop this?"

"On Earth, chlordane was banned in the late twentieth century. Since then several scientific solutions to the problem have been tried with great success. When I return to Earth, I'll put your case to the Interplanetary Health Organization. They will probably be willing to fund the cleanup of the pollution and monitor the health of your people."

"Will it take a long time?"

"I'm not sure, but it's a fairly massive undertaking by anyone's standards, don't you think?"

Marcus bowed. "I appreciate your help more than I can say." He gestured to his Council members. "We will all do our best to aid any attempts to rid our planet of this blight." A roar of affirmation resounded through the chamber. As the men filed out, Sven came up behind Marcus and slapped him on the back.

"The small white-haired woman might be old but she is definitely feisty. I would enjoy a night in her bed."

Marcus fought a smile. "If she is correct about saving our planet, I'll ask her if she'll consider it."

"Your consort might not agree."

Marcus turned slowly around to find Douglass waiting for him. In her soft brown uniform she looked different, more in control, less passionate. He noted the circles under her eyes and the lines of strain around her mouth.

Marcus stopped smiling.

"You are no longer my consort. I released you from that vow."

"So you did, and a good thing too."

By Odin, why didn't she simply stick a knife in his gut and disembowel him? It would be much cleaner. He tried to turn away but she caught his wrist.

"I think I deserve better. I think the title future wife might suit."

He set his teeth. "I grow weary of your humor. I am well aware of my lack of children and wife."

"Then you have given up hope of ever having a child?"

His words caught in his throat. "Doctor Jensen has already told me Lillian's child cannot be mine. As you heard, I intend to make provision for her and her family and offer a dowry to the man who created the child with her. But I will not marry her and claim another man's child as my own. Do you think me so desperate?"

Douglass stamped her foot. "Marcus, there's no need to poker up. You know that's not what I meant." She drew in a breath. "Will you please listen to me? If you want me to stay, I will. I love you."

A roaring sound filled Marcus' ears as he stared at her. She was willing to stay with him and give up any chance of future children? For a heartbeat he considered dragging her into his arms and never letting go. But what did he have to give her? A planet on the brink of destruction and no hope of a normal family life?

"I cannot ask you to do that, consort."

She studied him, her mouth set in a tight line. "You've already decided what I want and what is best for me have you? Is that your last word on the subject?"

He couldn't speak. Didn't she understand that he was doing this for her own good? Couldn't she see that it was the hardest thing he had ever had to do?

She reached up and touched his cheek. He could feel the fine trembling in her fingers. "I see. You'd rather wait and find your broodmare rather than trust in my love."

He had to walk away from her and stare out of the window. He gripped the windowsill. "You can't stay here."

"Then you don't ever wish to see me again?" He turned back to meet her furious gaze and she stalked toward the door. "Fine! See if I care! Be all noble and heroic and kingly and...stupid!"

The door slammed behind her, leaving Marcus alone. He reran the conversation in his head. What had he missed? Deep down she must know that he loved her and was letting her go for all the right reasons.

Footsteps sounded outside and Sven flung open the door. He scowled at Marcus, drew back his fist and hit him in the jaw.

When Marcus recovered from the explosion of pain that rocked him back on his heels, Sven still blocked his path.

"I regret the necessity of saying this, Sire, but are you a complete fool? Why did you let her go?"

Marcus rubbed his jaw and glared right back at him. "Because it is not safe for her to remain on this planet, you know that."

"So you will let her go back to Earth and marry another man because she thinks you don't care about her?" Sven spat on the ground.

"I do care, but..." Marcus stared at Sven. Would Douglass really come back? Would she be prepared to wait until his planet was free of contamination? He remembered his words to Lillian above love being a gift and that she shouldn't turn away from it. Damn, why hadn't he thought to tell Douglass that he loved her and then ask her what she wanted to do instead of deciding for her? She was worth more to him than any potential child. Sven was right, he was a fool.

Galvanized into action he wrenched open the door and sprinted down the stone steps to the courtyard. Sven followed him. An empty cloud of dust greeted his arrival. He caught hold of one of the stable hands. "Where is the crew of the *Eagle One*?"

The man pointed toward the spaceport. "They've about to leave, Sire."

Marcus swore. "Get me a *wulfrun* and hurry!"

Douglass gathered her possessions from the space hotel. They were few enough. She bit her lip and reminded herself that she carried the best memory of her time on

Planet Valhalla within her own body. She didn't really need anything else.

Marcus didn't want her.

Perhaps it was her own fault for not being upfront about the baby. She thought her declaration of love would be enough. Had she expected him to pull her into his arms and demand that she marry him and be damned to the consequences? Somehow she had, romantic as that was. All she'd needed to know was that he loved her first and foremost regardless of whether she could give him a child or not.

Obviously she'd miscalculated. Men were so dense sometimes. Marcus had decided to be noble. Some shocked part of her hadn't expected his desire for a child to be stronger than the love she believed he had for her. She glared at her distraught face in the mirror. God, she wasn't going to cry anymore, she wasn't. How dare Marcus be such a good, kind, thoughtful, irritating asshole?

It was time to remind herself how lucky she was. She had a good, steady job, a son who needed her and friends who liked her company. Compared to most people she was blessed. She'd had an out-of-this world erotic vacation which she would remember for the rest of her life, and she'd begun to realize that all men weren't like Danny's father. Some of them really did value women and children.

She touched the *ozan* blossom she'd tucked into her bag. Its heavy scent reminded her of Marcus' warm skin after they made love. Despite all her doubts, she'd finally met the right guy. He just happened to be in the wrong place at the wrong time and on the wrong planet.

Harlan knocked sharply on the open door, his dark hair shining in the sun.

"Consort, the captain says to tell you they are ready to depart."

Douglass picked up her bag and walked toward him. His arms closed around her. He kissed the top of her head and placed a thick gold necklace around her neck. "May the gods keep you safe, consort. I will miss you."

She raised her face to study his. "If the gods are good, Harlan, you might soon have a family of your own to think about and you'll soon forget all about me."

His expression gentled. "I'll never forget you. Your body in its gloriously aroused state will haunt my dreams for my lifetime."

Douglass patted his cheek and headed out the door. Bron waited there for her. His sweet smile made her want to cry again.

He kissed her on the mouth. "Goodbye, consort. Thank you for sharing your body with me. It was an honor I shall never forget."

"Thanks. Bron. It was my pleasure." She looked over his shoulder hoping to see Sven but there was no sign of him. Typical that her two favorite men had better things to do than see her off.

She spotted Marge at the entrance to the ship's cargo hold and waved. In ten more minutes, Planet Valhalla would be nothing more than a speck in the inky blackness of space. After a deep steadying breath she made her way up the gangplank. She looked down at Bron and Harlan who stood waiting at the bottom and waved. A cloud of dust rose at the entrance of the spaceport, reminding her of her first moments on the planet when Marcus had arrived to rescue her.

"Douglass, wait!"

From her vantage point, Douglass saw Marcus and Sven as they galloped into the port on two sweating *wulfruns*. Refusing to go down to him, she waited for Marcus at the top of the stairs. He dismounted with fluid grace and ran up the steps toward her. His fur-lined cloak rippled in the wind and exposed his muscular chest.

His golden eyes blazed in his face as he sank to one knee in front of her.

"Douglass, will you be my wife?"

Douglass hugged her arms to her chest as if her heart might leap out of her rib cage. "You told me to go. You said you didn't want to see me again."

He looked up and fixed his gaze on her. "I lied. I find I'm not that self-sacrificing. If the planet becomes free of toxins, will you come back and be my wife?"

"And if it doesn't?"

He sighed. "Then my planet will die and my people will have to find somewhere else to live." He got to his feet. "Whatever happens, they will still need a queen. And even if they no longer want me to lead them, I would be content by your side."

She tried to imagine him getting a job on Earth and living quietly in her apartment. Somehow she couldn't picture it and she didn't want him to change too much. He was born to be a king; he had the skills and the intelligence of a ruler. Was she prepared to compromise and go with him and his people if he took them to a new planet?

"Any woman would be glad to be your queen." After all the tears she shed over him she refused to make it easy.

He held her gaze. "But there is only one woman I love."

She swallowed hard. Dammit, why did he have to be so appealing and downright sexy? "If I become queen I'll be making some changes around here."

Sven, who had come up behind Marcus, snorted. Douglass glared at him.

"We can discuss that, love. I am more than willing to consider your opinions."

To her surprise, Marcus looked sincere. She smiled. The poor guy. He had no idea of the extent of her plans to bring his people, especially the females, into the twenty-fifth century.

"I'll marry you, Marcus."

He gripped her hands, his face a blaze of joy. "Now?"

She glanced around and tried to locate Marge. A crowd had grown around them. Her friend was caught behind Sven, trying to push her way past.

"Captain, do we have time to get married?"

Marge nodded. "If you can make it quick. I can log it on our ship's records as well as on this planet's. Then it will be all official." She grinned at Douglass. "I'll go and help Sven rustle up the Valhalla equivalent of a pastor. Congratulations, pal, or should I say, Your Majesty?"

Douglass scarcely heard her, her gaze locked with Marcus', her hands grasped firmly within his.

"I love you, Douglass." His quiet words were for her alone. She wanted to cry again as happiness bubbled through her. "I'll wait for your return, however long it takes."

She smiled into his eyes. "You can come and visit me and Danny on Earth, you know. I'm sure our son would love to meet you."

He chuckled, the sound low in his throat. "No, he won't. I'll just be someone that distracts his mother. But I will work hard to become his friend and his father if that is his wish."

She pressed his hand to her stomach. "That's very sweet of you but I didn't mean my son. I meant *your* son."

Marcus went still. "I do not understand."

"I think you do."

"My *son?*"

Marcus fell to his knees and wrapped his arms around her waist. He kissed the slight swell of her abdomen, his voice sounded choked. "You have given me everything I ever wished for. With this precious gift to look forward to, I will certainly come and visit you on Earth."

When he looked up at her, tears fell down her cheeks. His eyes radiated a fierce joy she had never experienced before. It made her feel like a goddess. He got to his feet, keeping her hand in his.

"I will send Sven, Harlan and Bron with you to Earth to take care of you."

Douglass frowned. "I don't need to be cosseted, Marcus. Having a baby is a perfectly normal event."

His mouth set in a familiar hard line. "If I cannot be there, I wish your servers to take my place. Surely as my queen you will be expected to have servants?"

"I have a two-bedroom apartment, pal. Where will they all sleep?"

Marcus raised an eyebrow. "With you, of course, how else will they be able to service your needs and protect you?"

Douglass stared at him. "They can't do that on Earth. I'd end up in all the tacky papers as some kind of sex fiend! And I have a child who lives with me."

He smiled at her. "We will discuss this after our marriage, consort. We will—what is it you say—reach a compromise."

He nodded decisively. "Aye, I will speak to the captain about this before you leave and ask if I might contact the government officials on Earth. If your planet recognizes mine as a sovereign nation, you will be treated like a queen.

They will be obliged to protect you and provide suitable living accommodation."

Douglass stopped smiling. "I thought you said we would compromise?"

He looked surprised. "I am. If it was up to me, I would insist you took twenty-four of my bodyguards with you and were protected night and day."

She poked him in the chest with her index finger. "As long as I'm on Earth, I'm going to live the life I'm used to. I'll pay my own bills, I'll keep my apartment and I'll continue to go to work."

He touched her cheek, his expression tender. "I admire your courage and I understand that you have had to be self-reliant to bring up your child alone. But the fact that you have agreed to be my wife, and you carry my child, will change things." He hesitated. "I have the means and the desire to make your life easier, to share your responsibilities and bear some of your burdens; will you not allow me to do so?"

She stared at him for a long while as the preparations for their hasty wedding went on around them. It would be hard for her to relinquish some of the control she'd fought to establish over her life and harder still to trust him with her heart and with Danny. But he'd said he was willing to give up his planet and his people for her. He was prepared to meet her halfway. If she truly loved him, could she offer him anything less?

She took a deep breath. "I love you, Marcus."

He kissed her mouth. His unique taste and scent made her want to cling to him forever. "We will learn to please each other, consort. We will learn to live in harmony with our children."

His quiet confidence made her want to cry. Before she could reply, Marge reappeared with Thorlan at her side. "This guy says he can do it, okay?"

The entire crew of the *Eagle One* spread out below the staircase, joined by the curious planet dwellers, a sea of colors and faces turned up to the spacecraft. Sven, Harlan and Bron stood on the steps like three gigantic bridesmaids. All of them were smiling, whether at the prospect of traveling to Earth or purely for the joy of seeing their king married, Douglass couldn't quite say.

Marcus bent close to murmur in her ear. "When you return to Valhalla we will hold another more private ceremony in the ancient temple. I look forward to seeing you displayed and aching for me, your cream flooding your sex, your nipples hard and sensitive to my fingers and mouth."

Douglass shuddered. "Let me have the baby first, and then I'll let you know whether I ever want you near me again."

He looked thoughtful as his gaze drifted over her body. "You will want me."

Thorlan cleared his throat as Marcus' satisfied gaze fell on a blushing Douglass.

"If you would like to stand beside the king, my lady, we will begin the ceremony."

When Douglass stared into Marcus' eyes, the unorthodox setting for her wedding disappeared from her thoughts. They'd fight, for sure but she knew, without any doubt, that her future life as Queen of Valhalla would never be described as boring.

# Epilogue
## *Earth, seven months later*

&

"Are they all with you?"

The admissions nurse swallowed hard as she tried to keep her gaze on Douglass who waited impatiently in front of the desk, arms crossed over her huge belly. Douglass looked over her shoulder. What was the problem? The guys all had white shirts, leather pants and boots on, so they looked respectable. Sven had Danny on his shoulders, Harlan and Bron were on either side of her mother and Marcus was…where was Marcus?

Another contraction ripped through her and she grabbed hold of the desk.

"Of course they're with me. Why else would they be here?"

Sven tapped her on the shoulder. "Don't forget your breathing, My Queen. It will ease the pain."

Douglass glared at him and then returned her gaze to the nurse who was smirking at Harlan. "Excuse me? Can you just admit me? I don't want to have my baby in the hallway."

The nurse blushed and checked her screen. "Name please?"

"Blood Axe," Douglass said through her teeth. Where the hell was Marcus when she needed him? And why did she feel so stupid having to call herself Mrs. Blood Axe? She should have registered in her maiden name.

Another contraction crashed over her and she almost bit through her lip.

"Are you sure you are registered here?"

Douglass placed both her hands on the desk. "Of course I am. Do you think I'm doing this for fun?"

"Excuse me, My Queen, but I believe the teacher at the birthing class said you should try and maintain your serenity for the sake of the baby," Sven murmured close to her ear.

She swung around to face him. He took a step back, his face blanching. She pointed at the door. "Take my mother and Danny somewhere quiet and find Marcus—now."

"Is Bloodaxe all one word or two?" asked the nurse.

Douglass closed her eyes. Two strong hands came around her and supported her weight.

"Blood Axe is two words and there is no need to worry about registering my queen," Marcus said. "I have just spoken to the hospital's chief administrator and my wife is already cleared to proceed."

"I'm not a spaceship," Douglass murmured. Trust Marcus to go to the top. He kissed her cheek.

"No, you're not but I'm sure you'd like to get on with having our child."

Douglass opened her eyes to see her husband smiling down at her. She was so glad he'd been able to get here for the birth. He'd been with her for four weeks this time and wasn't planning on returning to Planet Valhalla for a good long while afterward. Thanks to the hard work of the Interplanetary Health Organization, the cleanup process on the planet was going well. The contaminated soil had been removed and the people were receiving the best treatment available to recover their health and fertility. A delighted Marcus was busy planning for their return.

She tried to relax as Sven reappeared and reported that her mother was settled with Danny in the waiting area. She'd made all her servers take the birthing classes alongside her, just in case they were needed, but things had worked out just fine.

"Oh my god, you're that Viking king from the stars, aren't you?" The nurse shrieked and clapped her hands over her mouth. Douglass glared at her. How typical that the nurse should only recognize the Blood Axe name when she saw Marcus. In the past few months, news of their "space romance" had leaked out and they had become the topic of several lurid articles in the *Intergalactic Enquirer*. Despite the size of San Francisco and even with state-of-the-art security, it had proved impossible to hide four strikingly handsome Vikings and a visibly pregnant woman. Thankfully Douglass saw her obstetrician approaching and they were able to walk away before the nurse asked for an autograph.

Sven, Harlan and Bron followed after her, their expressions purposeful. She glanced up at Marcus as another contraction shuddered through her. He held the door of the birthing room open for her.

"Do you want them to stay outside?" Marcus asked.

She glanced back at her servers' hopeful faces and sighed. "Oh come in, you've experienced everything else with me, why should you get to miss out on the fun part?"

The delivery room seemed to shrink as everyone crowded inside. As another contraction swept through her, she gripped Marcus' fingers until he winced. Despite the pain, a sensation of peace settled deep within her. Her new child would know who his father was and he would always be loved. Surrounded by the men who had taught her about pleasure and allowed her to rediscover love, she prepared to welcome her son into the world.

*Enjoy an excerpt from:*
LOGAN'S FALL

Sharra trembled, alone in the receiving room. Her pulse raced as she quivered with shock. It was *him*! The Karn'alian warrior was the stranger whose dreams haunted her night after night, tormenting her with jumbled images of explosions, two bloody women, a little boy and *him*, superimposed against the disturbing revelation of pain and heartbreak. She'd seen his nightmares and shared his physical pain.

Now she understood why her attempts to secure passage out of Zalian Three had been unsuccessful. It hadn't been easy, but she'd managed to convince her guards to allow her to wander around the trade zone yesterday. As she'd pretended to peruse the wares of intergalactic merchants, she'd quietly inquired about paying for transport off the planet. There hadn't been a vendor or cargo ship operator who'd been willing to take her. It was now clear why the gods hadn't allowed her to escape. She wouldn't have met *him* had she been able to leave.

The initial shock of seeing the man from her dreams faded. In its place was a calm acceptance, a deep-seated certainty that their lives were intertwined. Fate had brought him to her, though what role she would play in his life was unknown to her. It just felt *right*.

His appearance in her life was no accident. Her destiny was tied with the Karn'alian warrior.

Footsteps echoed through the chamber. Sharra whirled around. *He* stood a short distance away, dressed the same as he was earlier, minus the stiff military jacket. A thousand butterflies fluttered inside her stomach. Her breath caught as their eyes met, a wave of recognition slamming into her. This man was no stranger. She knew his dreams, his thoughts and his pain. *Kismet.* Destiny was at hand.

His eyes were dark and unfathomable as they swept over her. Sharra trembled, trying to maintain her composure in the face of his intimidating presence. He was big, well over six and a half feet, taller than any Zalian male she knew. His hair was short and thick, the color of a clear, starless night. It set off the deep green of his eyes, reminiscent of a lush forest. His nose was straight and proud, his jaw square, a perfect foil for his firm, unsmiling lips. A soft shirt molded his massive chest, outlining a taut, muscled body that appeared no less menacing than the weapon holstered at his side. Overall, his countenance was grim, daunting. Forbidding.

"I'm Logan." He ventured closer. "Hello, Sharra."

A strange, syrupy warmth seeped into her skin, penetrating clear to her soul. Her nipples tightened, reacting to his proximity. Sharra inhaled deeply, disconcerted.

"Don't be afraid," he murmured gently.

He stood so close she caught his clean, masculine scent. This near, his visage was less harsh, the striking features appearing almost handsome.

Logan's lips tilted at the corners. "Are you not able to speak?"

Sharra caught her breath at the smile that transformed his whole face. "I-I can speak fine."

"How old are you?"

"Five and twenty."

"How do you feel about being given to me?"

A shiver slid down her spine at the faint possessiveness in his voice. "It is my duty to obey the Lord Marshall."

"You are willing?"

His eyes were beautiful, darker flecks of green surrounding the lighter irises. Sharra pulled some air into her lungs in a bid to relax. "A single, unprotected woman in Zalian society has very limited options. Since my parents' death, I have no family left. The Lord Marshall placed me in his son's household in order to provide me with some measure of protection."

"As a sex slave?"

Sharra tore her gaze away. "Zalian men like to collect things. The more money and power they have, the more women they can bring into their household. I was fortunate to be given the protection of the Lord Marshall's name." She lifted her chin, trying to discern feelings of disgust or disparagement from him, but detected nothing. He wasn't easy to read. When he remained silent, she tilted her head. "You're surprised by the Zalian way of life?"

"I've seen stranger things. Are you willing to settle on my home planet of Karn'al?" he asked abruptly.

*Yes. I belong with you now.* That certainty was tempered with apprehension at the thought of going with him to Karn'al, where she would run a greater risk of being found out. An empath in their midst would not be welcomed or accepted. "I have no wish to be the cause of a diplomatic problem. My place is with you now."

"And what is your opinion about being given to me?"

"I'm not opposed." Sharra dared to look at him directly. The sensuality etched in the sharp angles of Logan's face ignited a fiery ripple of awareness in her body. She understood completely what being given to him meant and all that it implied. She was hardly a simpering virgin.

"And will you be forthright enough to tell me the truth about yourself?"

"W-what truth is it you speak of?"

"That you find no enjoyment in the act of mating."

Heat crept up her neck. "Who told you that?"

His gaze was quietly assessing, missing nothing. "It's true then?"

An'ric's doing, she supposed. Sharra hadn't bothered to refute the crass, careless statements he'd made in public. Letting people believe she was frigid suited her purposes. Men generally didn't like to bother with women like that.

"Take off your clothes."

# Why an electronic book?

We live in the Information Age—an exciting time in the history of human civilization, in which technology rules supreme and continues to progress in leaps and bounds every minute of every day. For a multitude of reasons, more and more avid literary fans are opting to purchase e-books instead of paper books. The question from those not yet initiated into the world of electronic reading is simply: *Why?*

1.  *Price.* An electronic title at Ellora's Cave Publishing and Cerridwen Press runs anywhere from 40% to 75% less than the cover price of the exact same title in paperback format. Why? Basic mathematics and cost. It is less expensive to publish an e-book (no paper and printing, no warehousing and shipping) than it is to publish a paperback, so the savings are passed along to the consumer.

2.  *Space.* Running out of room in your house for your books? That is one worry you will never have with electronic books. For a low one-time cost, you can purchase a handheld device specifically designed for e-reading. Many e-readers have large, convenient screens for viewing. Better yet, hundreds of titles can be stored within your new library—on a single microchip. There are a variety of e-readers from different manufacturers. You can also read e-books on your PC or laptop computer. (Please note that Ellora's Cave does not endorse any specific brands.

You can check our websites at www.ellorascave.com or www.cerridwenpress.com for information we make available to new consumers.)

3. *Mobility.*   Because your new e-library consists of only a microchip within a small, easily transportable e-reader, your entire cache of books can be taken with you wherever you go.

4. *Personal Viewing Preferences.*   Are the words you are currently reading too small? Too large? Too… ANNOYING? Paperback books cannot be modified according to personal preferences, but e-books can.

5. *Instant Gratification.*   Is it the middle of the night and all the bookstores near you are closed? Are you tired of waiting days, sometimes weeks, for bookstores to ship the novels you bought? Ellora's Cave Publishing sells instantaneous downloads twenty-four hours a day, seven days a week, every day of the year. Our webstore is never closed. Our e-book delivery system is 100% automated, meaning your order is filled as soon as you pay for it.


   Those are a few of the top reasons why electronic books are replacing paperbacks for many avid readers.

   As always, Ellora's Cave and Cerridwen Press welcome your questions and comments. We invite you to email us at Comments@ellorascave.com or write to us directly at Ellora's Cave Publishing Inc., 1056 Home Avenue, Akron, OH 44310-3502.